Borgel

Borgel

by Daniel Pinkwater

Macmillan Publishing Company   New York

Macmillan Publishing Company
866 Third Avenue, New York, NY 10022
Collier Macmillan Canada, Inc.
First Edition
Printed in the United States of America

10 9 8 7 6 5 4 3 2 1
The text of this book is set in 13½ point Bembo.

Library of Congress Cataloging-in-Publication Data
Pinkwater, Daniel Manus, date.
Borgel/Daniel Pinkwater.—1st ed.   p.   cm.
Summary: Melvin recounts his extraordinary adventures in time and
space with his 111-year-old sort of great-Uncle Borgel.
ISBN 0-02-774671-2
[1. Space and time—Fiction.   2. Humorous stories.]   I. Title.
PZ.P6335Bo   1990   [Fic]—dc20   89-13421   CIP   AC

To Harlan Ellison,
who keeps trying to help

(1)

This is how Borgel turned up. I don't remember any of this myself. It's the story the family tells. Nobody quite knew who Borgel was. There was some vague idea of him, but neither my parents nor anybody else could remember having seen him. There was an old aunt in Cleveland, Ohio, who knew all about the family, and who was related to whom, but she had died years ago. There was nobody left who remembered much—for example, no one remembered for sure where we originally came from. I assume it was someplace in Europe, but no one knew exactly where.

The family name didn't provide much of a clue—Spellbound. Spellbound is an English word. English Borgel certainly was not. Where he came from I never found out. He had an accent. He came from the Old Country. That's what he called it. He never said which old country.

Borgel turned up one day with thirty-two large, lumpy, black valises. He brought them in a taxicab. My mother was home alone at the time.

"Missus Spellbound?" he asked when my mother came to the door.

My mother said yes, she was Mrs. Spellbound.

"Congratulations!" Borgel said. "You are going to be allowed to take care of an old man. God will like you for this."

Then he carried his thirty-two valises up the stairs, two at a time. He refused to accept any help. After he had brought all the valises up to the apartment, he asked if he could have a cup of hot water. My mother was in a state of something like shock. She didn't know who this old man was, and she couldn't understand why she had allowed him to carry thirty-two large leather valises up the stairs and to send the taxi away. She had even offered to help him carry the valises.

"No thank you," Borgel said with an accent. "When I have to have a woman help me carry thirty-two valises up three flights of stairs, I will lie down and die—which I am not ready to do yet, thanks God."

My mother led Uncle Borgel to the kitchen and put the kettle on. "Hot water, you said?"

"Yes, beautiful Missus," Borgel said. My mother liked that. When my mother poured the hot water into a cup and placed it in front of Borgel, he took an old-fashioned purse out of his coat pocket. My mother thought he was going to offer to pay for the hot water, and was about to tell him that it was not necessary, but what he took out of the purse was a tea bag, which he swished in his cup a time or two, squeezed out, and then returned to the purse.

"I won't be any trouble," he said.

At this point my mother screamed. She said it surprised

her that she screamed suddenly like that. She said she had felt a scream coming on for a while, and it just suddenly got out. It didn't have anything to do with the tea.

What she screamed was, "Who are you anyway?"

"You didn't get my letter?"

"What letter?"

"The letter I sent you."

"I didn't get any letter!" My mother was still screaming. It didn't seem to bother Borgel.

"So you didn't get the letter. What does it matter as long as I'm here, right?"

"I don't know who you are!" my mother shouted. "Who are you?"

"That's easy," Borgel said. "I'm Borgel. I'm your relative."

"Borgel?"

"Borgel."

"You're my relative?"

"Yours or your husband's—I'm not clear about which."

My mother had stopped screaming. Now she was repeating everything Borgel said. "Mine or my husband's and you're not sure which."

"That's right," Borgel said. "Do you remember the old aunt, the one in Cleveland, the one who died?"

"Yes."

"Well, she probably knew. I never paid attention to things like that. The important thing is that I'm here, right?"

My mother felt numb all over. "Right," she said.

"A hundred and eleven," Borgel said.

"A hundred and eleven?" my mother asked.

"How old I am," Borgel said. "A hundred and eleven years old. I could go anytime. It's nice of you to take me in."

"I have to call my husband," my mother said.

"Sure," Borgel said. "How is he anyway, health okay?"

"He's fine," my mother said.

"Good. I'm glad to hear that. Which is my room? I may as well put the valises away."

That was how Borgel came to live with us. There was some more discussion, of course. My father came home from work early, and he and my mother talked with Borgel.

Borgel had a little to add to what he'd said already, but not much. It appeared that his old apartment—he referred to it as "the old apartment" in "the old building" in "the old neighborhood"—was slated for demolition. Somehow he knew that we were his only living relatives, so he came to live with us.

He wasn't specific about how he was related to us.

"What's the difference how I am your relative?" he asked. "I am your relative, and I am a hundred and eleven years old, and you have to take care of me—what could be simpler than that?"

Borgel had already moved the thirty-two valises into the little spare bedroom at the back of the apartment. There wasn't much more to say.

All this happened when I was quite small. I don't

remember any of it. At that time, my world wasn't as big as the whole apartment. I don't remember when I began to notice that Borgel was around. He continued to live in the little room, and he continued to give his age as a hundred and eleven, year after year.

I have an older brother and sister, Milo and Martha. They were and are more or less perfect. Honor students. Extra good manners. Religious. Boring. I only bring up their names in the interest of accuracy, because I feel I should mention everyone then living in the apartment.

Obviously, Uncle Borgel wasn't a standard uncle. He was more along the lines of a great-great uncle, or a second cousin of my father's grandfather, or something like that. We called him "uncle" because that was the best we could think of. It seemed to satisfy him.

Occasionally my parents would have conversations about him. "Of course I feel sorry for him," my mother might say. "It's too bad they tore down the building he lived in to make room for the new sewage treatment plant—but is this the right place for him? I mean, wouldn't he be happier in one of those communities they have for older people?"

This conversation would be taking place in the living room. From nearly a hundred feet away, back next to the kitchen, behind a closed door, over the sound of the television, over the sound of Milo practicing the French horn in his room, would come a shout that everyone in the apartment could hear clearly.

"Phooey!"

"That was a coincidence, of course," my father would say.

"Of course," my mother would say.

And they would drop the subject for another few months.

Frequently, Uncle Borgel would not come out of his room for two or three weeks at a time. The second bathroom was in the hall right outside his door, and he could dart in and out without being seen—at least he never was. My mother said that sometimes she could hear a blender working in Borgel's room, and sometimes she could smell cooking. Evidently, he had a hot plate in there.

In the beginning she would worry about Borgel, and knock on the door and ask if everything was all right. Borgel would answer that everything was fine, and please not to bother about him. He never opened the door.

The only member of the household to see the inside of Uncle Borgel's room for the first few years was Fafner the dog. From the day Borgel arrived, Fafner spent almost all his time there. Uncle Borgel would open the door a little and let Fafner out when it was time for a walk—that is, when Borgel didn't take him himself. When Fafner came back, he would sit outside Borgel's door and whine until he was allowed in.

On a couple of occasions, I remember hearing growling and scuffling and happy barking coming from the room. They were wrestling.

My mother reported to us that while everyone was

away at school and work, Borgel would come out of his room. He would have his hat and coat on. He and Fafner would go out for two or three hours. When they came back, Fafner would appear to be tired. My mother thought they were going for long walks.

One night, Borgel appeared in the living room where we were all watching TV. He pulled a straight chair into the middle of the room, and sat with his back to the set.

My mother said hello to him. He bowed from his chair. She asked him if he would like a cup of hot water, tea, or perhaps a cookie.

"No thank you—I just had an eggplant," he said.

One Saturday afternoon—maybe I was ten or eleven—I ran into Uncle Borgel. I was just hanging around, not doing much of anything, when Uncle Borgel suddenly appeared. He had a way of doing that. One second he would not be in the room—and then he was.

"Okay, sonnyboy," he said, "answer me this—what is an *eft*?"

"It's a lizard, isn't it?" I said. "Like a salamander."

"HO-kay," Borgel said. "Now, what is a *wok*?"

"That's a Chinese frying pan."

"Prew-ty good," Borgel said. "Now tell me, please, Mr. Smartypants, what is a *roc*?"

"It's a big bird," I said. "Sinbad the Sailor met one in the story."

"Bingo!" Borgel shouted, and handed me a dime. Then he went to his room.

The next day, I received a letter. It was an invitation.

To Mr. Melvin Spellbound:

You are invited to visit me in my room
after supper tonight.

Borgel

Wear a tie.

I later got to know that one could only visit Uncle Borgel's room by invitation. Walking up and knocking on the door was no good. The invitation might come hours, minutes, or weeks in advance. It would read

You are invited to visit me in my room
at seven o'clock on the first of June.

And wear a tie.

The invitations always ended with "wear a tie." When I visited Uncle Borgel, with my tie on, for the first time, I found him sitting in a room crowded with valises and suitcases—the ones he had arrived with. They were all made of dull, scuffed-up black leather with bumps on it. They were stacked almost to the ceiling, and I could see more of them through the partially open closet door. In addition to the suitcases and Borgel, there was a bed, two chairs, an empty bookcase, and a framed photograph of a man with a bushy beard wearing a big cowboy hat. There was nothing else visible in the room.

Apparently, Uncle Borgel kept all his possessions in those suitcases, and took things out as he needed them, putting them away afterwards.

"Hello, Melvin," Uncle Borgel said. "Would you like a cup of Norwegian vole-moss tea?"

"I've never had any," I said.

"So you'd like to try it," Uncle Borgel said. He opened a valise, and took out an electric hot plate, a couple of cups, and a kettle which turned out to be already full of water. He put the hot plate on top of the bookcase and plugged it into a wall socket.

"It will be ready in a few minutes," he said. "Sit there." He pointed to a chair. I sat.

"Good! Now—a surprise quiz!" he said.

"Huh?" I said.

"Wait for the question," Uncle Borgel said. "No guessing—besides, 'huh?' is not an answer. First question: What is an *asp*?"

"It's a little snake—a poisonous one," I said.

"Hooray! Ten points for that one!" Uncle Borgel said. "Now the second question—what is a *boa*?"

"A boa is a big snake—a boa constrictor."

"Right again! You didn't make an asp of yourself that time. Here comes a tricky one. What is a *fry*? Take your time."

I took my time. "A fry is a . . . baby fish?"

"Whoopee! You got them all, Mr. Genius. A perfect score!" Borgel dug out a dime and handed it to me.

"Excuse me," I said. "Why do you do that?"

"Do what?"

"Only ask questions about three-letter words?"

"I don't know—I just happen to like three-letter words today. There are a lot of big topics with only three letters—God, for example, and Art, and bugs."

"*Bugs* has four letters."

"Bug then—look, the water is boiling already. I'll get the teapot."

Uncle Borgel took a teapot from the suitcase, shook some horrible-looking gray leaves into it, and poured in boiling water.

"There are more kinds of bugs than anything, you know," he said, "except stars in the three-letter *sky*."

I couldn't decide whether the Norwegian vole-moss tea tasted more like moss or vole—never having tasted either to my knowledge. It wasn't exactly bad, but it was very strange.

"The Laplanders drink this like Grepis-Cola," Uncle Borgel said. "It's good for the brain and other muscles."

"What's Grepis-Cola?" I asked.

"It's the seventy-fifth most popular soft drink in the world," Uncle Borgel said.

That interested me. I like topics like that. I already knew the twenty most popular soft drinks in the world. I thought I would make a point of asking Borgel sometime what the other fifty-four were.

"Okay!" Uncle Borgel said. "Now it is time for the musical entertainment. I hope you like music."

"Sure, I like music," I said.

"You like Beethoven?"

"I'm not sure," I said. Classical music was a topic I didn't know very much about. Nobody in the family cared much about music, classical or otherwise—unless you counted Milo, but he only played French horn in the high-school band because things like that are supposed to look good on your college application. He already wanted to become a dentist and drive a German sports car. I don't think he was any good as a French hornist.

"Beethoven is a first-class genius," Uncle Borgel said. "He's maybe as good as the human race can produce. If you listen to the music he wrote, you'll find out things about yourself. If you listen to music by Beethoven a lot, you will never become stupid—unless you already are, in which case there's still no harm in it."

Uncle Borgel got a radio out of a suitcase. It was made of wood. He unplugged the hot plate, and plugged in the radio. There was a friendly light in the dial, like a Christmas tree light.

"This will take a minute to warm up," he said. "I watch the newspaper to see what is going to be on. Tonight they are playing Symphony number five. It's just right for a boy who doesn't know Beethoven. It's exciting. You'll probably like it."

He was right. It was exciting, and I did like it. The music made me feel the way I did when I watched certain adventure movies—better in a way, because the feeling was inside me instead of being connected with a story on the screen.

While listening to Beethoven's Symphony number five, I also got to like Norwegian vole-moss tea.

When it was over, I asked Uncle Borgel, "Would you invite me the next time something by Beethoven is going to be on?"

"Of kee-ourse!" he said.

I got to be invited to Borgel's room more often than anyone else in the family.

My parents were practically never invited. Milo and Martha visited him occasionally, but they appeared to regard it as charity—being kind to an old man, part of their perfection program. I doubt that Borgel had much fun with them, but he'd invite them from time to time so they could feel virtuous.

I visited Borgel at least once a week. We listened to the radio, drank cups of Norwegian vole-moss tea, and had discussions about all sorts of things. I would also go for walks with Borgel and Fafner. He liked to walk at a fast pace for fifteen or twenty blocks. It was hard to keep up with him. It was difficult to believe he was over a hundred years old.

Of course, Borgel saw the rest of the family, even though they didn't visit him in his room very often. He would pass through the apartment on his way out with Fafner—and at long intervals he would join the family in the living room, always sitting with his back to the television. It turned out that he disliked television because the people in the pictures appeared so small. He said it gave him the willies.

I wasn't able to find out from Borgel where the Old Country was. He would never say. I had developed a theory that it was one of those countries that don't exist anymore, like Bosnia or Herzegovina. Borgel only referred to it as the "Old Country." It didn't seem likely that he had forgotten. He didn't appear to ever forget anything.

He'd say things like: "See this button? It's a bone button. I remember when all buttons were made of bone, or shell, sometimes wood. There weren't any plastic buttons until Matthias Klopmeister invented a celluloid button-making machine in 1883."

Someone who remembers who made the first celluloid button-making machine, and when, isn't likely to forget where he was born, but Borgel never mentioned the place by name.

"Melvin," Uncle Borgel said to me, "some details are important, and some details are unimportant. I pay attention to the important ones."

I asked him if the history of button making was important.

"Of course buttons are important. Next to zippers, buttons are among the most important inventions of mankind. Imagine how much trouble getting dressed and undressed would be if you had to deal with strings and pins and knots and such."

I asked Borgel what some of the other important inventions of mankind were. He said they were underarm deodorant, window screens, long-playing records, and Chef Chow's Hot and Spicy Oil.

I liked it very much when Uncle Borgel would let me come with him on visits to the Old Neighborhood. The Old Neighborhood was where Uncle Borgel lived before he came to live with us. He lived in the Old Apartment in the Old Building.

(2)

The Old Building wasn't there anymore. In fact, the Old Neighborhood was hardly there anymore. It was mostly a bunch of vacant lots. The apartment houses had been torn down to make way for a new sewage treatment plant that was never built. They tore down the Old Building (with the Old Apartment in it), filled in the basement with bricks and rubble, and left it that way.

Uncle Borgel didn't leave many traces. Assuming he was born in some defunct country like Herzegovina, it was interesting that he should have most recently lived in an apartment that wasn't there anymore, in a building that wasn't there anymore, in a neighborhood that wasn't there anymore. It isn't exactly accurate to say that the Old Neighborhood had ceased to exist entirely. There were still a few buildings standing, and the main business street, Nemo Boulevard, was not quite dead. That was where Uncle Borgel and I would go when we visited the Old Neighborhood.

Uncle Borgel said the Old Neighborhood was the only place in town where you could get a bottle of Chef Chow's Hot and Spicy Oil. It's one of the essential ingredients in most of the cooking Borgel did. He bought a bottle of Chef Chow's Hot and Spicy Oil at least once a month. I asked him why he didn't buy it by the case and save trips. He told me he liked to go back and visit the Old Neighborhood—and besides, it would be dangerous to keep many bottles of Chef Chow's Hot and Spicy Oil together in one place.

"Safety first," he said.

Another thing Uncle Borgel liked to do when we visited Nemo Boulevard was to go to the Star Spangled Banner All-American Cafeteria. The Star Spangled Banner All-American Cafeteria was Uncle Borgel's favorite place to hang out. It was a place where not a word of English was ever heard.

Whenever we went there, he would have two or three glasses of coffee. They served it in thick, barrel-shaped glasses. Uncle Borgel would put a lot of milk in his coffee and stir it with a spoon. He would also eat a rhinoceros roll. A rhinoceros roll is an ordinary hard roll. In some places they call them kaiser rolls, or kimmelwicks, or stale-o's. At the Star Spangled Banner All-American Cafeteria they called them rhinoceros rolls.

When we went to the Star Spangled Banner All-American Cafeteria we would usually meet Uncle Borgel's friend Mr. Raspelnootzpiki.

Mr. Raspelnootzpiki was also very old. He claimed to be even older than Uncle Borgel, but Borgel said he was probably not even a hundred yet. When they met at the cafeteria they would speak in some strange language. It was unlike anything I had ever heard. It sounded as though they were clearing their throats, but they were communicating.

I asked Uncle Borgel a trick question, hoping to get a clue about where he had come from: "Is the language you speak with Mr. Raspelnootzpiki the language you spoke in the Old Country?"

"No. Mr. Raspelnootzpiki doesn't come from my Old Country."

"Is his Old Country anywhere near yours?" I was still hoping to get some information I could use. I could look up Mr. Raspelnootzpiki's Old Country in an atlas and see what countries were nearby.

"His country was next door to mine."

I was really getting somewhere.

"What is the name of Mr. Raspelnootzpiki's Old Country?" I asked.

Uncle Borgel made a sound. At first I thought he was preparing to spit, something he did better than anybody, but I realized he was saying the name of Mr. Raspelnootzpiki's Old Country.

"How do you spell it?"

"In English?"

"Yes. How do you spell it in English?"

"You can't spell it in English."

Mr. Raspelnootzpiki wore a thick black overcoat, winter and summer, and he smoked horrible, cheap cigars. He also wore thick eyeglasses and a funny slouch hat. He and Uncle Borgel would alternately talk and listen.

I would sit, sipping my coffee and nibbling my rhinoceros roll, and wonder what they were talking about.

Another reason I liked to go to the Old Neighborhood with Uncle Borgel—in addition to sitting around in the Star Spangled Banner All-American Cafeteria with him—was that I liked the stories he told on the bus. Sometimes he'd tell true stories from his own life, about climbing a mountain in Asia, or being a cowboy in Brazil, or sailing in the South Pacific. Other times he would tell a story about some criminal, and how the police caught him. Halfway through many of these stories, I would realize it was the plot of a television program the family had watched the night before while Borgel sat with his back to the set.

Very often he'd tell stories from the Old Country. They were nursery stories or folktales. They were all about animals. At the end of each story, he would pause— then he'd say "moral," and then he'd tell the moral.

Here are some of his stories:

The Story of the Rabbit and the Eggplant

Once upon a time there was a race between a rabbit and an eggplant. Now, the eggplant, as you know, is a member of the vegetable kingdom, and the rabbit is a very fast animal.

Everybody bet lots of money on the eggplant, thinking that if a vegetable challenges a live animal with four legs to a race, then it must be that the vegetable knows something.

People expected the eggplant to win the race by

some clever trick of philosophy. The race was started, and there was a lot of cheering. The rabbit streaked out of sight.

The eggplant just sat there at the starting line. Everybody knew that in some surprising way the eggplant would wind up winning the race.

Nothing of the sort happened. Eventually, the rabbit crossed the finish line, and the eggplant hadn't moved an inch.

The spectators ate the eggplant.

Moral: Never bet on an eggplant.

The Story of the Mole that Thought It Was a Fox

There was a mole that was unusually large and beautiful—for a mole. It was stronger and faster than all the other moles. It decided that it must not be a mole at all.

"A terrible mistake has been made," said the mole. "I have been raised as a mole, when all the time I have been a fox."

The mole told all the other moles, and all the other animals, that it was really a fox.

"Is that a fact?" said all the other animals, none of which had ever seen a fox.

One day, a real fox passed through the part of the forest where the mole that thought it was a fox lived.

"I am a fox," said the mole to the fox.

"Well, you sure are an ugly one," said the fox, and continued on his way.

Moral: Who cares?

The Story of the Fish that Thought It Was Drowning

A fish in a forest pool called out to the animals that passed by, "Help! Help! Help me out of here! I'm drowning!"

An elk spoke to the fish, "You're not drowning. You are a fish. You live in the water. If you were to come onto dry land, you would die."

"Oh," said the fish.

Moral: Don't listen to anything a fish says.

The Moose and the Squirrel

In olden times, everybody knew that the moose was a great trickster. The moose always played jokes on the other animals, and cheated them, and got them into trouble. So, when the moose came upon the squirrel, who had collected a great number of nuts for the winter, the squirrel resolved to have nothing to do with him.

"Oh, squirrel," said the moose, "why don't you let me put all those nuts of yours in my pocket? I'll take them wherever you like, and you won't have to run back and forth with one nut at a time."

"Oh no," said the squirrel, "you'll play some sort of trick on me."

"No I won't," said the moose, "I'll just put your nuts in my pocket, and take them wherever you say."

"Oh no, you'll cheat me," said the squirrel.

"No I won't," said the moose.

"Oh no," said the squirrel, "you'll get me into trouble."

"No, honestly," said the moose, "I just want to help you."

"Really?" asked the squirrel.

"Sincerely," said the moose.

"All right, I'm going to trust you," said the squirrel. "You may put my nuts in your pocket."

"I just realized," said the moose, "I don't have a pocket. Let's forget the whole thing."

Moral: Animals are stupid.

Of course, stories like that would have appealed to me much more when I was a lot younger, but I still liked to hear Uncle Borgel tell them. He was a good storyteller. He'd imitate the animals, and sometimes—if he was telling about a squirrel, for example—he'd get up and hop around the bus, imitating a squirrel. He really got into the spirit of whatever he was telling. Sometimes everybody on the bus got involved.

(3)

One night, Uncle Borgel tiptoed into the room I shared with my brother, Milo. We were both asleep. Uncle Borgel pressed a flashlight and a scrap of paper into my hand and then tiptoed out. I switched on the flashlight, and read what was written on the sheet of paper:

> *Come to my room in one hour. Get dressed,*
> *and carry your shoes in your hand. Also*
> *bring some extra clothing—a spare shirt,*
> *underwear, socks.*
>
> *Don't make any noise.*
>
> > *Borgel*
>
> *Tie not necessary.*

I waited until the luminous hands of the alarm clock indicated that three-quarters of an hour had passed. Then I got up, dressed in the dark, rummaged around for some spare clothes, and carrying my shoes in my hand, made my way through the dark apartment to Uncle Borgel's room.

"Come in."

I went in. Uncle Borgel had on his hat and coat. He

21

was sitting on his bed with one of his lumpy leather valises on his lap.

"Thanks for coming," he said. "I just wanted to say good-bye."

"Where are you going?" I asked.

"I thought I'd take Fafner with me. It would be too cruel to leave him here. He wouldn't understand."

"You . . . you're . . . you're going?"

"Yes. Going."

I didn't know what else to say, so I said, "Why did you ask me to bring these extra clothes?"

"It's cold in the apartment. I thought you might want to put them on. Do you want to put them on?"

"No. I don't want to put them on."

"If you're tired of holding them you can put them in this valise." He opened the valise. "Here, put them in the valise."

I put my clothes in the valise.

"Well," Uncle Borgel said, "I will be going now. Come, Fafner."

"Wait," I said. "You're just going to wander off in the middle of the night? I mean . . . just leave?"

The truth was, I was a little worried that maybe Uncle Borgel had gone crazy. I couldn't just let him wander off like that.

"If you're going, I'm going with you," I said.

"That's okay by me," Uncle Borgel said. "I'll wait while you put your shoes on."

I laced my shoes, grabbed my coat from the coat tree in the hall as we passed it, and followed Uncle Borgel in his long black coat and broad-brimmed hat, carrying his black lumpy leather valise and followed by Fafner, down the stairs, out of the building, and into the street.

This was my situation: I was out in the street, in the middle of the night, with the family dog and my sort-of great-uncle who was at least a hundred and eleven years old. What it amounted to was that we were running away from home.

It was very strange. I had overheard conversations between my parents about the possibility that Borgel might go soft in the head sometime. This didn't seem to be very likely in Borgel's case. He always did the crossword puzzle with his leaky fountain pen in under two minutes. Once I got him as a present a book of the world's hardest crossword puzzles. He did them all in about half an hour.

Borgel could also figure in his head faster than I could work my father's adding machine. And he could juggle five balls.

Still, it seemed very odd, this taking off in the middle of the night. Probably the right thing to do would have been to wake up my parents and tell them Uncle Borgel had gone crazy and was running away. I couldn't do that. He was my favorite relative. If Borgel was going to run away, the only thing to do was to run away with him and see that nothing bad happened to him.

I myself had no particular reason to run away from home. I wasn't mistreated or anything of that kind. On the other hand, it occurred to me that there was no strong reason not to run away. I was fairly bored by my family, except Borgel. There wasn't anything better to do. But it seemed to me that I was entertaining foolish thoughts—after all, how far could we get? It would probably all come to nothing within a couple of hours.

Borgel was making his way along, peering at the parked cars. He was sort of mumbling to himself. I considered offering to carry his valise for him, but he never allowed that sort of thing. We went a block, turned the corner, went another block, turned another corner. We were going around the block! Borgel was obviously confused. Maybe he had gone soft in the head after all.

He continued to peer at parked cars. I couldn't imagine what he was up to. Then he put down the valise, opened it, and took out a length of stiff wire—a straightened-out coat hanger. He worked the wire into the window frame of a beaten-up old sedan, fished around, and caught the door-lock knob with the hooked end of the wire.

It only took a few seconds. "Get in," he said. Fafner jumped in. I followed him.

Uncle Borgel had broken into a parked car! Now he was fiddling around under the dashboard with another piece of wire—this time it was insulated electrical wire. He was hot-wiring it! Uncle Borgel was a car thief!

"Uncle Borgel, are you sure this is a good idea?"

"Sure. It's the only way."

"Suppose the police caught you and threw you in jail?"

"Ah-ha! Hypothetical questions! So what? What could they do to me—give me life in prison? Besides, I'm a cute old man. No court in the world would convict a cute old man. Anyway, I haven't done anything to get arrested for."

"Haven't done anything? What do you call . . . ?"

"Shhh! I have to concentrate."

Uncle Borgel felt around under the dashboard, poking with his piece of wire. Suddenly the engine turned over. Borgel smiled.

"That's got it," he said. The engine was coughing and sputtering. Borgel stamped on the gas pedal. The car vibrated and lurched forward. We were moving. We were criminals. I was an accessory to grand larceny. I knew this because I had watched a lot of police shows on TV. Grand theft auto was what I was an accessory to—a felony. I thought you could get about seven years for that.

Not being a cute old man, I figured they'd throw the book at me. I wasn't feeling very happy. Uncle Borgel obviously was. He was singing as he drove.

Uncle Borgel had often cautioned me not to be a wimp. He was of the opinion that the rest of the family had wimpish tendencies, and had warned me against falling into those ways. I bring this up because I do not want to give the impression that I was unaware of the thrills and excitement available to persons who have committed Grand Theft Auto. I appreciated that we were taking a lot of risks, and I could see that it was a sort of adventure— but my thoughts kept returning to the prospect of getting caught and thrown into prison.

The old sedan chugged onto the interstate, and in fifteen minutes or so had worked up to cruising speed. I was thinking that if one commits Grand Theft Auto and then crosses a state line, it becomes a federal crime, and one stands a good chance of being machine-gunned by the

FBI. I considered working this into the conversation, but I couldn't be sure whether it would have the effect of discouraging Borgel or just making him happy.

Fortunately, there wasn't much traffic on the interstate at that time of night—just the occasional convoy of trucks, which would shoot past us and be out of sight in two minutes. I began to cling to the hope that we would get so far away from the scene of our crime that nobody would be looking for us. When we got to a city, I'd persuade Borgel to dump the car, and we'd go home on the bus.

Oh no! The state line was coming up fast! We'd be across it soon! This was it—the big time—professional crime. It was going to be death in a hail of bullets for me.

"Melvin, look in the glove compartment and see if there are some whole wheat fig bars in there." I had to hand it to Uncle Borgel—he was a cool one thinking of fig bars at a time like this. I opened the glove compartment and rummaged around.

"A Super-Yeast candy bar, raisins—anything you find in there," Borgel said. "I'm feeling hungry, and I don't want to stop until we've burned up this tank of gas."

I found a cellophane bag of whole wheat fig bars and passed it to Borgel.

"Care for one?" he asked.

"Maybe later," I said. I was examining something else I'd found in the glove compartment. It was a plastic folder containing a card. It had Uncle Borgel's picture on it. I could read the card by the light of the tiny bulb in the glove compartment. It said that the car was a 1937 Dorbzeldge sedan, that it had four cylinders and weighed 5,307 pounds, and that it was owned by Borgel MacTavish. MacTavish was Borgel's last name—not that he was a Scotsman; MacTavish was as close as any English-speaking person could come to pronouncing his last name, which sounded nothing like MacTavish, but even less like anything else.

"This is your car," I said.

Borgel sprayed whole wheat and fig crumbs all over the dashboard. "Naturally it's my car. What did you think, that I stole it?"

"Why did you break in with a coat hanger, and start it without a key?"

"Because I lost my key after I had the car about a year, and then the country where she was made went out of business, so I couldn't get a new one. How about this car? Forty-five years I've had her and never changed the oil once. She's a honey!"

Honey was making about forty miles per hour and clouds of white smoke. I took a bite of a whole wheat fig bar and settled back against the seat cushions.

"This is the life!" Uncle Borgel said. "The open road, a good machine, and a whole wheat fig bar! By the way, see if the dog will eat one of those."

I offered Fafner a fig bar, which he accepted without enthusiasm. He didn't like food that got stuck in his teeth.

"This is the life all right," I said. "By the way, are we going any place in particular?"

"Yes, we are!"

"Do you feel like telling me where?"

"I feel like telling you a story from my life."

"Will we be gone long?"

"That depends on what you call long. We'll see."

"I was just thinking about my parents."

"I left them a note."

"Oh, that's good. What did the note say?"

"The note said, *Melvin and I have gone away. We took the dog. Don't anybody go in my room. Love Borgel.*"

"That should do it," I said.

"Sure," Borgel said.

It sank in. We really had run away, Borgel, my hundred-and-eleven-year-old super-great-uncle, or whatever he was, and I.

"There are some bottles of natural honey-sweetened ginger beer in the back," Borgel said. "See if you can reach a couple."

I hung over the seat back and felt around. Under Fafner, I found a brown paper bag that clinked. I reached in and fished out two bottles of ginger beer.

"What do I do with these?" I asked.

"Give them here," Uncle Borgel said. "Pardon my teeth."

With his teeth he pried the cap off one of the bottles, and handed it to me. He did the same with the other bottle, and spat both caps out the window. I was impressed.

The natural honey-sweetened ginger beer tasted good and sort of burned my lips. I liked the sensation of hurtling along in the old Dorbzeldge, driving through the night with Borgel and snacking on good things.

"How come you never mentioned having this car?" I asked him.

"There are lots of things I've never mentioned. I don't use the car for little errands—just for big road trips. That's why she's lasted so long."

"When was the last time you took a road trip?"

"Nineteen hundred and forty-six," Borgel said. "I ended up in Yellowstone."

"Are we going to Yellowstone?"

"I wasn't planning on it—but you never know. We'll see some interesting things, that's for sure."

"Going to drive all night?"

"Until I get tired. You can go to sleep if you want to."

"I'm not sleepy."

"So I'll tell you a story from my life."

Uncle Borgel didn't say anything.

"Okay," I said.

"Okay, what?"

"Okay, tell me a story from your life."

"I'm picking one out."

More silence.

"Do you mind if I play the radio?" I asked.

"Go ahead, I'm still picking."

I turned the knob. A green light behind the dial came on.

"Give it time to warm up," Borgel said.

In a minute or so I could hear static. I twisted the tuning knob. I found a station. A man was talking. He sounded like someone. He sounded like Borgel's friend Mr. Raspelnootzpiki. He was speaking that same language. "Hey!" I said.

"Shortwave," Uncle Borgel said. "This car's got everything."

"He's talking in that same language you speak with your friend!"

"No, he's not. That's French."

"That's not French."

"You can speak French?"

"No, but . . ."

"So how do you know it isn't French?"

"Because it doesn't sound like French."

"The announcer has a cold and a Canadian accent. He's talking French. You can believe me. I know a lot."

It didn't sound like French. It sounded exactly like Mr. Raspelnootzpiki. Borgel's mind was made up. There was no point in arguing with him.

On the other hand, he could have been right. I was getting pretty sleepy. At one point I thought I heard the announcer say something about the Star Spangled Banner All-American Cafeteria, but by that time I was already drifting into sleep as the Dorbzeldge thundered along the highway.

"Okay."

"Okay, what?"

"Okay, I've picked the story from my life, the one I want to tell you."

I shook myself awake. "Okay, tell it."

"Okay, so here goes. Long ago in the future, in the galaxy of Witzbilb, near Terraxstein—"

"Long ago in the future?"

"Who's telling this story? Be quiet and pay attention."

"Sorry."

"Long ago in the future, in the galaxy of Witzbilb, near Terraxstein, a planet with five moons, on a little planetoid no bigger than a gob of spit in this vast and expanding universe, there was a moment."

"A moment?"

"That's right."

"This story is about a moment?"

"Absotivlutely."

"A moment, like a moment in time, right?"

"Right. Now to continue, this was a happy little moment that had never done anybody the least harm. This moment, whose name was Dennis, played with the other little moments, romping and gamboling with never a care in the world. Little Dennis never suspected that he would become a moment in history—of course he already had, because this is a story of the future told in the tense of the past."

"Would you mind if I went to sleep now?"

"This isn't holding your interest, is it?"

"I'm nodding."

"Okay, how about if I told you the true story about how I became a time tourist?"

"A time tourist? What's that?"

"It really should be time-space-and-the-other—that's

the element in which I am a tourist—but time tourist sounds better. It could be a story on TV. 'Borgel the Time Tourist.' 'Borgel the Time Tourist and His Amazing Adventures.' 'The Amazing Adventures of Borgel the Time Tourist.' Welcome to another thrilling episode of 'Borgel, Tourist in Time.' A watch company could sponsor it.

"The makers of Psycho watches brings you another episode of 'Borgel the Time Tourist.' Hello, I am wearing the Psycho 640-kilobyte digital watch, just like the one Borgel the Time Tourist uses. It runs in all directions, and underwater, and at temperatures up to 16,000 degrees centigrade—and you can hit it with a hammer—you can leave it in the freezer—you can spit on it, you can stomp on it—nothing's gonna hurt this baby. Bullets you can shoot at it—acid, magnets, vibrations!"

"So what's a time tourist?"

"I'm one. I'm a time tourist. Me."

"Yes?"

"Yes. As I said, it would be better to say space-time-and-the-other tourist, because it isn't only time, you know."

"What's the other?"

"Ha! That's easy, sonnyboy—it is that which exists in neither time nor space. It's the best part of being a time tourist."

I had read some stuff along these lines, and I had seen plenty of science fiction on television, so this sort of thing was not new to me. Neither was it new for Uncle Borgel to incorporate plots of television shows into the stories he told me. The way to enjoy this was to play along.

"So what do you do when you're a time tourist?" I asked.

"Well, the first thing you need is a vehicle. This Dorbzeldge is a first-rate time-space-and-the-other machine. The next thing, if you really know what you're doing, is to have some good traveling companions. You and Fafner have the makings of the very best fellow tourists."

"So I'm a time tourist, too."

"You are now."

"What else do we need?"

"Just the willingness for it to happen, that's all."

"The willingness for what to happen?"

"The willingness to leave one time-space-and-the-other continuum and enter into another. Are you willing for that to happen?"

"Sure."

"You've got to be really willing. You can't just say so to be polite. Are you really willing? You really want to take the trip?"

"Yes, I really want to."

"HO-kay! We've got everything we need, and we're started! Whoopee!"

The night sky was clear and full of stars. I looked at Uncle Borgel. He was happy. There was a big smile on his face, and it was possible to see a few of the stars through his head.

That's neat, I thought, Uncle Borgel is sort of translucent. I held my hand up in front of the windshield and looked at some stars through it. They were dimly but plainly visible.

"Hot cha!" Uncle Borgel shouted. "Time-space-and-the-other, here we come!"

I came all the way awake. "Wait a minute! I can see through my hand! What's happening?"

"You have a problem, Mr. Adventurer?" Uncle Borgel asked.

"I can see through my hand! I'm transparent! What's going on?"

"Relax. It's normal."

"It's not normal! I can see stars through my hand!"

"Sort of neat, wouldn't you say?" Borgel asked.

"Except that it's terrifying. What is this?"

"Now, don't be a weenie," Borgel said. "What kind of time tourist do you call yourself if you get all excited just because you see a few stars?"

"I'm seeing these stars through what I hope is solid flesh, and I want to know why."

"Why? I don't know exactly why. It's something that happens when you travel very fast through time-space-and-the-other."

It was sinking in. Borgel wasn't just telling me a story from television. We really were traveling through time and space—or something of the kind. I was squinting through the palm of my hand at stars, and it was like looking at them through a pair of sunglasses.

"What else happens? Tell me everything."

"All sorts. Sometimes we become completely immaterial—sometimes we turn into heat, sound, light. All sorts. It's fun."

"This is dangerous, isn't it?"

"This is no more dangerous than eating ice cream—"

I felt a little better.

"—in a hot air balloon in a high wind."

I felt a little worse.

"Don't worry," Uncle Borgel said. "I've been doing this sort of thing for maybe eight or nine hundred years. It's a snap. You'll get used to it."

"What do you mean, eight or nine hundred years?"

"It's just a guess. I lost track of myself a long time ago."

"You're telling me that you're eight or nine hundred years old?"

"Older—you can't become a time tourist where I come from until you're all grown up. You're lucky you don't come from there."

"From where?"

"From the Old Country. Where you have to be all grown up before you can be a time tourist. There aren't many boys your age have an opportunity like this."

"I feel sort of sick."

"The fig bars didn't agree with you? Have another swig of the ginger beer."

"Uncle Borgel, I'm not following this very well. Maybe you'd better start from the beginning."

"Sure. We've got plenty of time. A story from my life. You're comfortable?"

"No, I am not comfortable. I am confused and scared, and I can see through my hand, not to mention through your head. Up until a few minutes ago I was under the impression that we were riding along an ordinary road in an ordinary stolen car. Now you tell me that we're traveling through time-space-and-the-other, and that you're more than nine hundred years old. None of this makes me comfortable."

"Well, you seem to have all the facts straight. Maybe I can help you feel a little better about this if I tell you some history."

"Uncle Borgel, anything you can do to help will be greatly appreciated."

"Fine. Now settle back, look at the nice stars through your hand, and I'll tell you everything. The first thing you have to understand is that time is not like a string."

"Time is not like a string?"

"Some people think it is. It isn't. It also isn't like a series of frankfurters, a loop, a figure eight, a fast train, a fast train with a mosquito in it, a melting ice cube, a floppy pocket watch, a French cookie, rotten apples, Silly Putty, or Swiss cheese."

"No?"

"No."

"So?"

"So, *time* is like a map of the state of New Jersey—not like the state of New Jersey or even the state of New Jersey seen from the air, or from a satellite—it is like a *map* of the state of New Jersey. Got that?"

"Sure."

"Okay, next is *space*. Space is sort of like a bagel, but an elliptical one, with poppy seeds. You got that?"

"Got it. Time is like a map of New Jersey. Space is like a bagel."

"Good. Next is *the other*. This is the hardest to explain.

The best I can do is that the other is like a mixed salad in which there is only one ingredient you like. Now, one more time."

"Time is like a map of New Jersey, space is like a bagel with poppy seeds, and the other is like a salad with only one thing you like in it," I repeated.

"Excellent. Have a fig bar. Now I can get on with the history."

"Am I allowed to ask questions?"

"Soitainly."

"Why is time like a map of New Jersey?"

"A good question. This is why time is like a map of New Jersey: Let's say you are in Newark, New Jersey, and you want to go to, oh, let's say Perth Amboy, New Jersey. You don't know exactly where Perth Amboy is. What do you do?"

"I look at a map?"

"Preezacktly! You look at a map. And the map shows you what roads to take to get to Perth Amboy, or Hoboken, or Elizabeth, or anywhere in the state. Now, here comes the big question. If you were in Newark and were thinking about Perth Amboy, would Perth Amboy exist?"

"Sure."

"Right. Now, let's imagine you're still in Newark, and you are *not* thinking about Perth Amboy. Would it still exist?

"Yes."

"And if you had never even heard of Perth Amboy, and weren't thinking about it—would it exist then?"

"Yes."

"How about Jersey City?"

"Same thing."

"Keereckt! It is exactly the same thing. So, Mr. Professor of Philosophy, all the towns and cities and places in New Jersey exist, whether you know about them or are thinking about them or not, right?"

"Right"

"Trenton?"

"Yes."

"Hasbrouck Heights?"

"Yes."

"Weehawken?"

"Yes."

"Cape May Courthouse?"

"Is there such a place?"

"There is."

"Then yes."

"So there you are in Newark, and all the other places exist even though you are not in them, see?"

"I do."

"The same thing with time. All the moments in time exist, even though you're only in one of them."

"I get it!"

"You do?"

"Sure. It's easy." I was getting sort of excited. "The points in time extend in all directions, and even though we can only know about them one by one, the others are all there."

"Perfect! Now if you left Newark and went to Moonachie, would Newark cease to exist?"

"No."

"And if you wanted to go back to Newark, would it still be there?"

"Probably."

"You're an intelligent kid."

"So if you have the means to do it," I said, "you can go back and forth from any point in time to any other point in time, because they're all always there, and it works out to be like a map of New Jersey or some other state."

"Wrong. Not some other state. Just New Jersey."

"Why not one of the other states?"

"They're the wrong shape."

While Borgel was telling me this, I was noticing that the road beneath us was starting to glow.

"The road is starting to glow," I said.

"That's normal," Borgel said. "Only a couple of things you need to understand before I can tell my story. You know about space?"

"You mean outer space, planets, and all that?" I asked.

"Space—inner, outer, near, far, solid, and immaterial; the distance between stars and the distance between an ant's ears and his hind foot—space, you know about it?"

"I know it exists."

"Good enough. You're a smart boy, Melvin. I'm glad I brought you with me. You know what is it light years?"

"That's the distance it takes light to travel in a year."

"So if we wanted to go to some galaxy that's 50 million light years away, and could travel at half the speed of light it would take us how long to get there?"

"I don't know. How long?"

"Too long, that's how long. That's space. But if you can move through time *and* space, both at once, and you sort of hit it diagonally, you can, in effect, get from Newark to Hoboken in about three seconds. That's how we travel in time and space."

"Sort of like a warp?" I asked.

"Oh-ho! We know who's been watching television," Uncle Borgel said. "Yes, that's the idea. So you should also remember from 'Star Trek' that if we change the angle a couple of degrees, we can leave Newark in the twentieth century, and hit Hoboken in the eighteenth. You still with me?"

"Still with you," I said. By this time there was no physical sensation of moving forward. Road vibrations, engine and tire noises had ceased, and the Dorbzeldge was completely silent. The road was now glowing a milky white, and to the sides of it was blackness. The only thing that told me we were moving was an occasional amorphous blob of light sliding past us. It didn't look anything like space travel on TV or a video game. What really surprised me was that the windows were still open.

"Are we traveling in time and space right now?" I asked Borgel.

"Full speed ahead," Borgel said.

"You know the windows are open."

"So? You're cold?"

"I mean, is it all right for them to be open?"

"Stick your hand out and see what happens." I stuck my hand out. It vanished—that is, it ceased to exist as I put it outside the car. I drew it back, and it reappeared.

"That's spooky," I said.

"Isn't it?" Borgel said. "Now are you ready to hear the story of how I became a time tourist?"

"One more question first," I said. "How does this Dorbzeldge work? Has it got phaser drive? Has it got warp drive? Has it got improbability drive?"

"It's got Hydramatic," Borgel said. "It says so right in the middle of the steering wheel."

(4)

"Back in the Old Country, when I was a boy, we used to sit around eating potatoes and telling stories about how mean our parents were. Sometimes we didn't have a bottle of Chef Chow's Hot and Spicy Oil to pour on the potatoes, and sometimes we did.

"That's how it was in my childhood. Not like today. Not like some places. My family was so poor and my parents were so mean that when I wanted to have a pet they gave me a peach pit. You getting this, Melvin? I wanted a little doggy, or a kitty, and they gave me a peach pit. And I loved that peach pit! I named it Lance. I taught it tricks and everything, but it was no use. We were too poor.

"Finally, my mother and father took Lance away and sold him to a rich family as a pet for their children. Can you imagine how horrible I would feel when I walked past the rich people's house and saw those children playing with Lance, who had once been my peach pit? Now, when I say these were rich people, I mean they had water. They had mud outside their house—we only had stones. And they only hit their children on the head instead of lunch. We got hit on the head instead of three meals a day.

Nobody was doing all that well in the Old Country.

"The finest thing any boy could hope to be was a time tourist. This was because a time tourist was permitted to leave the Old Country. In fact, everybody would help the time tourist, and give him things—you see, we wanted people to leave because that meant more room for everybody who stayed. Usually only the children of the extremely wealthy—families that had luxuries like clothing—could get to be time tourists. It was too much to hope for. All a boy like me could hope for was that maybe his father would knock a couple of his teeth out. But my father was too poor even for that—so what hope was there that I could become a time tourist?

"Still I had my crazy dream that somehow I would get to be a time tourist. When I was eleven years old, my father performed the ritual of throwing me out of the house and shaking his fist at me. This meant that it was time for me to begin my life's work, which in my family meant searching the fields for skunks that had been squashed under the hooves of the rich people's cattle. It was satisfying work, and after a year I found a skunk. This meant I could get married—but I didn't do that. Instead of trading the skunk's pelt for a bottle of Chef Chow's Hot and Spicy Oil, and going out looking for a wife, I went to the Great City.

"I traded the skunk skin for some Kleenexes, and I traded those for a pickle. It was the first pickle I had ever seen. I traded the pickle, and I traded what I got for the pickle, and I traded again, and I traded again. Every trade was a good one, and before long I was a prosperous man.

By the time I was nineteen I had a place to sleep indoors. When I was twenty-five I owned my own hat. Most people who had a hat had to share it with five or six other people. I had a hat strictly for my own use. I was going places, but I was still far from my goal of becoming a time tourist."

"You're making this up, right?" I asked Uncle Borgel.

"Every word. Why? You don't like it?"

"It's fine—I just wanted to ask you about that thing over there."

"What thing? You mean the big pulsating thing that looks like it's made out of light?"

"That's it. Is that anything we should worry about?"

"Only if it comes near us," Borgel said. "That's some kind of monster made out of energy. It might want to consume us."

"Consume?"

"Swallow us up. If it's one of those energy monsters, it eats everything it comes near—planets even."

The thing, the energy monster, appeared to be as big as the Sun. It was glowing a sort of peach color, tinged with green. It scared the dickens out of me.

"Uncle Borgel, I think it's coming closer. Is there any chance it doesn't see us?"

"Almost none," Borgel said. "It senses our electrical field. If we don't get away from it, we're in a lot of trouble."

"How do we get away from it?"

"Easy. We shift gears and go fast. This may feel strange. Just relax."

Borgel moved the gear selector lever. A red light began flashing on the dashboard. There was a high-pitched whine, and the Dorbzeldge began to vibrate, and then shake violently.

"Now I just give it the gas," Borgel said.

I felt a sensation in every part of my body. It was like being pricked with pins everywhere. The Dorbzeldge, and the space around it, began to glow with a white light. Fafner was whining uncomfortably in the backseat. I thought that the energy monster had caught up with us. Then, suddenly, we were enveloped in complete blackness.

"I can't see anything," I said.

"Guess how fast we're going?" Borgel asked.

"Too fast?"

"Three hundred seventy-two thousand miles per second. That's twice the speed of light, sonnyboy. I hate to go this fast—it's got to be bad for the tires. What's more, you never know where you'll end up. You carsick?"

"I feel weird. Do you think we've gotten away from that energy monster thing?"

"Probably it's centuries away by now—nawthing to worry about."

"So maybe we could slow down?"

"We're slowing down. You don't just step on the brakes after going double the speed of light."

The blackness had reduced to the sort of darkness I was used to. I still couldn't see anything, but I didn't feel as if we were inside a bottle of ink. Then, gradually, I became conscious of little points of light. The points of light became brighter, more defined, and I was able to perceive some of them as nearer than others. This looked like space as shown on TV.

"Where are we?" I asked.

"I have no idea," Borgel said. "I'm looking for a place to pull off the road."

"Road! What road? We're in outer space!" I shouted.

"What road? The Interstate, naturally. We've been on it all along."

If I squinted my eyes I could imagine that there was a sort of roadway looking like diamond dust or the Milky Way.

"Look," I said to Borgel, "I don't want to hear a story. I want you to answer my questions, one by one. Is that okay?"

"Sure thing," Borgel said, "but first let's pull off. I want a cold drink, and by this time the dog needs to stretch his legs."

"Pull off? Where?"

"Right here," Borgel said. He spun the wheel and the Dorbzeldge lurched to the right.

"A cold root beer in a frosty mug sound good to you?" he asked.

"It sounds fine," I said. I could see a large orange rectangle glowing in the blackness. There was some sort of writing on it, but the characters were like nothing I had ever seen—just a series of black and yellow squares.

(5)

"So get out," Borgel said.

I opened the door and started to put my foot out.

"Wait a minute! There's no ground!" I said. Beneath my sneaker there was nothing but velvety blackness, infinity.

"You can walk on that," Borgel said.

"No I can't," I said. "There's nothing there."

Borgel was chuckling. "Look, I'll get out and walk around to your side. There's nothing to be afraid of. It's as solid as concrete." Borgel walked around the car and stood by my open door. "Now, just put a foot out and feel."

I felt. There was something solid under my foot. I still hesitated. "How do I tell the difference between whatever this is and a big hole in space?" I asked.

"It's a knack," Borgel said. "After you've traveled in time-space-and-the-other for a little while, you'll just know when something is all right to stand on and when it isn't. You'll develop an instinct."

"What if I don't?"

"You will."

"Maybe I can't."

"Oom-possible. You develop instincts in order to survive—that's what they're for. Come over here."

Haltingly, I took a step away from the Dorbzeldge.

"Come right over here," Borgel said. He was standing by a long yellow object that ran along what would have been the ground, if there had been any. It appeared solid from a distance, but looked more like a beam of light when I got close to it. It resembled one of those concrete barriers in parking lots.

"Now . . . if you should step over this thing, then you'd be in trouble."

"Why?"

"Because there's nothing on the other side."

"Nothing to stand on?"

"You would just float away."

"Cripes! It looks exactly the same as this side!"

"Looks the same—but it's not the same. You have to sense which is which. Besides, they've got these markers all around."

What we were in WAS a parking lot. At the far end, under the glowing orange rectangle, was a structure made of some kind of shiny metallic stuff. A space-time root beer stand.

"Let the dog out," Borgel said. "He needs to run around."

"He'll fall over the edge."

"Dogs develop instincts faster than humans. Don't worry so much—you'll turn into an old man."

I opened the rear door. Fafner was asleep on the backseat. I called to him.

He bounded out of the car, gave a horrible shriek when he saw there was nothing but emptiness beneath him, and tried to turn in midair and scramble back inside. He hit the nonground and sprawled there. He lay still for a while, sniffing frantically. Then, gingerly, he got to his feet, and gave me a look of contempt.

"You blintz!" Fafner said. "You couldn't warn me?"

"The dog talked," I said numbly.

"Isn't this fun?" Borgel chortled. "They do that when you take them out in time and space. Some surprise, huh?"

I was feeling sick. Too much was going on. I was nauseated.

"I have to pee," the dog said. He wandered over to the barrier and lifted a leg.

"See," Borgel said, "how quick they develop instincts?"

"I love you," Fafner said to Borgel, and licked his hand. "Jerk!" he said to me. "Pee-wee! Dope! Stupid kid!"

In the midst of all this confusion I was suddenly confirmed in my lifelong suspicion that the family dog, Fafner, didn't like me.

"Now, how about some root beer?" Borgel asked.

"None for me, master—just some water—but you go ahead."

"I meant for Melvin," Borgel said.

"Oh," Fafner said.

We walked over to the root beer stand. Except where there was something—such as the stand itself, the Dorbzeldge, ourselves—there was nothing. The blackness above us was identical to the blackness below us. There appeared to be no source of light, but we and the things around us were plainly visible. This had the effect of making everything seem to glow with its own inner light.

The interior of the root beer stand was illuminated, and behind the counter was the single most disgusting thing I had ever seen or imagined. It was a formless pink mass with occasional tufts of coarse black hair, slimy patches, no eyes that I could see, and lots of red bumps and pimples.

"The proprietor is an Anthropoid Bloboform," Borgel said. "They're very industrious and clean—don't let appearances fool you."

An ugly hole opened in the repulsive mass, and an appropriately unpleasant voice came out, bubbling and rasping.

"My name is Alfred. I will be your waiter for tonight," said the Bloboform. "What may I serve you?"

"Two root beers in frosted mugs," Borgel said, "and a cup of water for the dog."

"No ice," Fafner said.

"That will be a hundred and twenty zlotys," said Alfred.

"Zlotys?" I asked.

"Common currency throughout the universe," Borgel said. "I have some."

"Any fries with that?" Alfred asked.

"He means French fried meteorites," Borgel explained, "a little heavy for humanoids. No thank you, Alfred. Just the drinks."

"It is my pleasure to serve you." The Bloboform

pseudohanded us our drinks, and we carried them to a wooden picnic table near the stand.

"I need this," I said. I took a swallow of my root beer. It was the best I had ever tasted. It was the first familiar thing I had encountered in the last hour or so, and it had the effect of calming me down.

"Now, look, Uncle Borgel," I said, wiping the foam off my upper lip, "don't you think it's time you explained a few things to me?"

"Sure. What's to explain?"

"Let's start with everything," I said.

"Awl-rightie!" Borgel said. "Here goes! I already explained to you about time, right?"

"Map of New Jersey," I said.

"Kee-reckt! And space also?"

"Like a bagel."

"Bingo! So now you want to know how it all works, and how we travel from time and place to time and place, and what all this is, am I right?"

"You are."

"Okeydokey! Now. You ever travel in a car, back on Earth and in your own time?"

"Of course."

"How does the car work?"

"How does the car work? It's got an engine."

"Yetz? And how does the engine work?"

"Well—you put gas in, and turn on the ignition, and I guess the gas burns up, or explodes, and the energy . . . uh, it gets to the wheels somehow and . . . uh . . ."

"Good for you! You know more about how cars work than I do. Me, I just turn the key, make sure the thing has gas, oil, and water poured into the appropriate holes, air in the tires, and I go. I don't know or care to know one thing about how the engine runs. When it breaks I take it to a mechanic. See?"

"You don't know how a car works?"

"No, I don't. Next, when you take a trip—ever been on a car trip?"

"Sure."

"And when you go on a car trip, you do what to make sure you'll get where you're going?"

"Well, you might look at a map—or you could just get on the road, and watch for signs . . . along . . . the . . . road. My God! You don't know any more about how any of this works than an ordinary . . .'"

"Tourist!" shouted Uncle Borgel. "That's it, son-nyboy! Oh, from experience I know a little about the people, sights, places, and customs—but as to theories, who cares? We're out to have a good time. Aren't you having a good time?"

"I'm having a good time, master," Fafner said.

"Good dog," Borgel said, patting his head.

"Hey," said Alfred the Anthropoid Bloboform, "you left your lights on." Borgel got up and walked toward the Dorbzeldge. When he was about ten steps from the car he was enveloped in a ball of orange light. Then he was gone. It couldn't have taken a whole second.

(6)

"What happened? Uncle Borgel? Where are you?" I shouted.

"Oh no!" the Bloboform said. "Not again!"

"Master! Where are you?" Fafner said. He was running in circles, sniffing the blackness.

"What happened? Where did Borgel go?" I asked Alfred.

"This is getting to be too much," the Bloboform said. "Nobody will come here anymore because of those darned kids and their bilboks."

"What are you talking about? What kids? What's bilboks? What happened to my uncle?"

"A bilbok is a gleep—you know, a gag, a practical joke—something that makes you go 'gleep!' Used to be you could buy bilboks in joke shops on Old Saturn 4 in the Fifth Age. Now they're prohibited, but those damn kids make their own, and work gleeps on people. I've got nothing against having fun, but maybe fifty customers of mine have been bilboked in the past couple of months. That sort of thing gets around, it can put you out of business."

"I don't understand a thing you're saying. I want to know what happened to Uncle Borgel!"

"Look. These kids, they come from rich families. They have their own time-space vehicles. They wander around playing gleeps and getting into trouble. They see your old uncle standing there, and they put a bilbok on him.

"That is, they subject him to an unstable transdimensional shifter. They move him—but no one can say where. He might be five minutes in the future, and all of a sudden we'll catch up with him, and he'll just be standing where he was—or he might be shifted six thousand years, and fifty billion light years, and maybe kicked onto another existential plane to boot. It's like tying someone to a rocket and just casually shooting the thing off. Now, don't cry, kid. You want a free root beer?"

"I'm starting to realize that I'll never go crazy, no matter what," I said, "because if I haven't lost my mind by now, it's never going to happen. Are you telling me that some kids passing by in some kind of spaceship . . ."

"A time-space ship," Alfred said. "They were probably here for a long time, but in our time continuum it was so quick that we never saw them."

"Okay, a time-space ship. Some kids just came along and zapped Borgel with some kind of . . . gleep . . . and now he's . . ."

"Gone."

"But not dead."

"Depends on where he landed—but not necessarily.

And, as I said, he might be nearby. The commercial bilboks they used to sell would just send you a few hours, and maybe a light hour at most. Usually. Maybe all your uncle has to do is call a taxi, spend a few zlotys, and he'll be back here in a jiffy, maybe a solar month."

"On the other hand . . ." I said.

"On the other hand, he might be gone for good. That's why those bilboks were outlawed. After a few years the humor starts to wear off."

I looked at the Bloboform. He was talking to me in a friendly enough manner. He was the closest thing to a friend I had at the moment. This did nothing to diminish his hideousness. It was, in fact, a sort of steadying element in conversing with him. I had to concentrate so hard on not throwing up that I escaped going into a panic.

"You say others have been, uh, bilboked here?"

"Many."

"And how many of them came back?"

"Two. That's two out of roughly fifty, or four percent. Your uncle stands a very good chance, considering that the chance of survival at all in this part of time-space is only about ten percent."

It was comforting to hear Alfred talk in this matter-of-fact way—even though it was nauseating in the extreme to watch him do so. I believe he was moved by my situation, and this caused him to quiver more than was strictly necessary and exude quantities of slime.

"Look, I'll make you a root beer float—with double ice cream—and you can sleep in that old Dorbzeldge while you wait for your uncle. And I'll give you free eats—he can pay me when he comes—and you can use my private bathroom, too."

This, when it came to the fact, was even more horrible than my imaginings at the moment, which were enough to bring on shudders. I went to talk it over with Fafner.

"The Bloboform says we can stay here."

"I heard, doofus. Dogs hear sixteen times better than humanoids. And if you spread out my olfactory membrane it would be as large as my whole skin."

"I'd like to do that," I muttered.

"I heard that, too," Fafner growled. "Now that you've gotten my master lost or killed—or whatever—are you going to take care of me or not?"

"You little crud!" I shouted. "How would you like me to kick your useless rump over that barrier and let you float around thinking over what a stupid, foul-smelling, ugly, offensive little cur you are?"

"Sorry, master," Fafner said. He gave my hand a dab with his tongue.

"Don't do that."

"Sorry. You going to feed me?"

"I'll talk to the Bloboform."

"I love you, master."

"Look, you hairy little cretin," I snarled. "I know you dislike me. Now, I'm going to make sure you have food, no matter how you speak to me. So stop with the hypocrisy."

"You mean it?" the dog asked. "You'll feed me?"

"Yes."

"No matter that I think you're a jerk?"

"That's right. I'm kind to dumb animals. Now shut up. I want to think."

"Ha."

"Of course, I may not feed you very often."

"I'll be quiet."

Alfred came out from behind the counter. I wished he hadn't done that. Looking at Alfred while he was more or less stationary was nasty enough. Watching him in motion was enough to make a dog gag—of which I had evidence.

"Here," he said, offering me a root beer float.

I wiped the slime off the mug.

"I'm kind of surprised that you speak English."

"Oh, you have to know languages in this business," Alfred said. "I get a lot of New York people coming through here."

As I sipped my root beer float, I was seized with an agonizing feeling of aloneness. I moaned into the mug, "Where can Uncle Borgel be?"

(7)

Borgel tumbled through blackness. He was unable to see, hear, or feel. He was not aware of having a heartbeat or breathing. He might have thought he was dead, except that the odds were against that—it never having happened before.

"What is this, a gleep?" he said.

Then there was light—a dim, unpleasant sort of light. Borgel found himself in a rocky and barren landscape. The soil was black, volcanic. It was cold. There were a few blades of grass.

Borgel had landed in an uncomfortable position. It was as though he were in the middle of a somersault, his shoulders flat, his body bent double, his feet over his head, his toes on the ground. He looked up at the gray, cloudy sky between his legs.

"Hmm," he said, figuring it out. "Hoop la!" He completed the somersault and bounced to his feet. "Not bad," he said. "Not many old guys over one hundred could do that."

Then he looked around. The dismal place was familiar. He had been there before.

"I've been here before," he said.

Borgel was pretty sure he knew where he was, but he held out hope that he had landed in Iceland, or some remote part of Greenland or Patagonia. There was always a chance he wasn't where he thought he was. But he was.

A fair-sized rock whizzed past his head. Borgel saw a gnarled and shabby figure standing on a little rise of ground. An old man—he was looking around for another rock.

Yep. I know where I am, Borgel thought.

"Giddadaheere!" the old man shouted.

"Daddy! Is that you? It's me, Borgel!" Borgel shouted.

"I know that," the old man shouted, hurling another rock.

"The Old Country," Borgel said, dodging.

(8)

Alfred must have been exaggerating about fifty of his customers having been bilboked in the past couple of months. Either that, or he calculated months differently, because he hardly had any customers at all.

Days—or what seemed like days—might go by with nobody stopping at the root beer stand.

"It's a lousy location," Alfred said.

Meanwhile, Fafner and I slept in Uncle Borgel's Dorbzeldge and waited.

Fafner was impossible. He complained all the time. We'd gone through the fig bars, and there was nothing Alfred sold that humans or dogs could eat except root beer floats. I was plenty sick of root beer floats, but Fafner was getting wild. It was starting to look as though he would eat me, or I would eat him.

Alfred turned out to be a nice enough guy. He spent his time puttering around the root beer stand. Sometimes, he'd let me help him—but really, there wasn't much to do.

I tried to get Alfred to tell me something about where I was, but he appeared to be almost completely ignorant.

He was interested in nothing but running his root beer stand, and talked about nothing but how bad business was. He didn't even remember where he came from. All he knew about was the root beer stand. It had been easier to get information from Uncle Borgel. I really missed him.

"Can't we call the cops or something?" I asked Alfred.

"Sure. We could call them. Two or three centuries and they might even turn up. And then what? Where would they look for your uncle? We're talking about infinite distances. I don't think you have any idea of what a lousy location this is."

We did ask the few customers who showed up if they'd seen Uncle Borgel. None of them had the slightest idea what we were talking about.

Incidentally, I got to see some pretty unusual life-forms at the root beer stand. We had some bean-people from Flamingus, clown-men from Noffo, and once a bus load of Freddians. It was interesting to see the different ways the various beings drank their root beer.

After a while, I was pretty depressed. I spent a lot of time hanging around the Dorbzeldge. Fafner spent practically all his time curled up on the backseat, complaining. Even though he was obnoxious, I felt more comfortable with him than with Alfred. He was closer to human.

Sometimes, we'd fool around with the radio, hoping to get some idea of where we were, or what sort of place it was—I still hadn't figured even that much out. We had no luck with the radio. When we could get a station, it was always in some language other than human. We got sick of listening to the gurgling, squeaking, and mumbling. Except for Michael Jackson records, they didn't play anything we could understand.

One day, I was rummaging around in the glove compartment at Fafner's insistence.

"Look," I told him, "we've been through and through this. There is nothing to eat in here."

"Look anyway," Fafner said. "Maybe there are some fig bar crumbs."

"I let you lick the crumbs out of the corners twice already."

"Look anyway. If I don't get something to eat soon, I'm going to die."

"You get root beer floats," I said.

"I'm sick of root beer floats! I hate root beer floats! I'm a dog! Dogs don't drink root beer!"

"There's ice cream in them," I said.

"Are you kidding?" Fafner screamed. "Licorice-flavor ice cream? Black ice cream? You think that's a treat or something? I'm your responsibility. You have to get me some real food."

"What do you suggest?"

"We could eat the Bloboform," Fafner said, craftily.

"Get real," I said.

"Okay, how about we eat the tires?"

We had been through this a hundred times. Fafner was going to list every single thing in our environment, from the root beer stand to my shoe, and suggest we eat it.

His other topic was the trunk. It was locked, and we didn't have the key. We had tried to pry it open with

Alfred's ice-cream scoop, but the Dorbzeldge was built like a vault.

"We could eat the upholstery," Fafner said.

"Shut up," I said. I had found something. Stuck to the back of a card advertising Sadie's Drive-Thru Fish Market in Columbus, Ohio, was a key! It was stuck to it with what looked like part of a melted cough drop.

"Looky!" I said, peeling the key off the card.

"Is that a cough drop? Gimme!" Fafner said.

"No, idiot. Look! It's a key!"

"We could eat this key?" Fafner said. He was still going through his endless list of uneatable things we might try to eat.

"It might be the key to the trunk," I said.

"And there might be food in the trunk!" Fafner was bouncing off the roof.

We raced around to the back of the car. It *was* the key to the trunk. I fitted it into the little slot, and turned it. The lock clicked. I raised the lid.

"There's food in there! There's food in there!" Fafner screamed. He was bounding around in circles.

I peered into the trunk. Fafner was standing with his front paws on the rear bumper. The trunk was full of all sorts of junk—including a twenty-five-pound bag of Kibblebitz Dog Food.

"Is that . . . ?" Fafner asked, drooling.

"It sure is," I said.

"That's dog food!" Fafner snarled. "It's mine! You can't have any. It's just for dogs. Mine!"

I slammed the trunk lid and put the key in my pocket.

Fafner's mouth snapped shut, drool dripping from the corners.

"I think I'll go over and see what Alfred is doing," I said.

"Of course, I'd be happy to share my dog food with you, master," Fafner whined.

"That's better," I said. "Get your bowl."

"Right away, master," Fafner said.

I would like to say, right here, that Kibblebitz Dog Food is tasty and nutritious. It is well-balanced, and easy to digest. I would recommend it to anyone—and it is very good with root beer.

I found something else in the trunk. It was the owner's manual for the Dorbzeldge.

(9)

Borgel stretched out on the flattened cardboard box, the place of honor in his father's house. "Must have been a bilbok," he said aloud to himself. "I suppose Melvin is still back at the root beer stand. Well, he's a capable boy. Besides, the dog will take care of him."

Old Blivnik, Borgel's father, spoke. "Borgel?"

"Yes, Daddy?"

"Sharrap!"

Same old Dad, Borgel thought. I have to get out of here.

(10)

I had a pretty good idea how to drive an ordinary car. I'd spent a lot of time behind the wheel of those miniature gas-powered racers at Riveredge Amusement Park at home. Reading the Dorbzeldge's owner's manual, I couldn't see that driving it would be much different.

My plan was to get Fafner and myself away from Alfred's time-space root beer stand, and maybe try to get home. Anything was better than waiting around there— and the truth was I didn't think Uncle Borgel was coming back. Or he might come back in fifteen or twenty years. I thought we ought to go while the bag of Kibblebitz was still pretty full.

Fuel was no problem either. I read in the manual that when the Dorbzeldge operated in time-space-and-the-other, it ran on Hydramatic drive, which was inexhaustible. The manual gave a few clues about the rules of time-space-and-the-other travel. In many ways, it was easier than operating a car at home on Earth in the twentieth century. It appeared that staying on the Interstate was something the Dorbzeldge would do automatically. There wasn't any need to steer most of the time, and you couldn't get lost—that is, you couldn't get any more lost than we were already. It would stay on the road, or the path, or the beam, or whatever it was. I thought I could handle it.

I talked it over with Alfred.

"Why do you want to leave?" the Bloboform asked. "Your uncle might come back any month now. Besides, I thought you were getting to like me."

"I do like you, Alfred. I just think we should go."

"Well, I wasn't going to tell you this, but I think you have a lot of talent for the root beer business. I thought maybe you'd stay and help me. When my time comes to transmogrify, you could have all this." Alfred made a sweeping gesture with a pseudopod, indicating the lonely, deserted, forlorn root beer stand.

"I'd like nothing more," I said. "But I really think we should go."

"Well, of course . . . if you think so." Alfred was really sad. "I'm going to miss you. Let's shake hands."

"Yich. I mean, before we do that, maybe you could tell me where we should go. I'd like to get someplace where I can send a letter, or maybe make a phone call. My family probably thinks I'm dead."

"Well, the Big City is probably your best bet."

"The Big City? How far is that?"

"Must be, oh ten or fifteen metaparasangs."

"Is ten or fifteen metaparasangs a long way?"

"Compared to what?"

"Never mind. What I want to know is, what sort of a place is it? Is it dangerous or what?"

"Well, you know—it's the Big City."

"You've never been there, have you?"

"Well . . . no."

"You're sure it exists?"

"Sure. Yes. Pretty sure. Sort of. I think so. Maybe."

"And it's in that direction?" I asked, pointing.

"To the best of my knowledge."

"That's good enough for me," I said. I started for the Dorbzeldge.

"Good luck!" Alfred shouted. He grabbed my hand. For a horrible moment, I thought he was going to hug me. "If your uncle shows up, I'll tell him where you went."

I slipped behind the wheel of the Dorbzeldge. Fafner was in the backseat, as usual, mumbling that I was going to get us both killed. "You can stay here with Alfred, if you like, until the kibble runs out."

"I'm going with you," Fafner said.

I remembered I didn't have a key. I stuck my head under the dashboard. There was a hunk of wire dangling down. I touched the loose end to various things until it made a spark. I heard the engine come to life.

I bobbed up and turned to Fafner in the backseat. "I got it started!" I said.

"Look where you're going, maniac!" Fafner shouted. "We're moving!"

We were heading for one of those barriers at the edge of the parking lot—on the other side was empty space.

I spun the wheel, and the Dorbzeldge turned. "According to the manual, we would have stopped automatically before going over the edge," I told Fafner.

"Did it ever occur to you that this thing might not be working perfectly?" Fafner asked. "I'd watch the steering if I were you."

"Good thought," I said. I maneuvered the Dorbzeldge out of the parking lot and onto the Interstate. It wasn't so hard to handle. As we picked up speed, I saw the root beer stand getting smaller in the rearview mirror. Alfred was waving his arm or something. We were on our way.

(11)

This is luck! Borgel thought. Only home a day, and what do I find? A skunk! Nice one, too. Hasn't been squashed more than a week. Well, I did it before—I can do it again.

From a neighboring field, old Blivnik shouted, "Hey! Borgel!"

"Yes, Daddy?"

"You founnaskung?"

"That's right, Daddy!" Borgel shouted, waving the prize over his head.

"Well, gerrahdaheere awreddy, y'bum!" Blivnik bellowed.

"All right, Daddy," Borgel called, with a tear in his eye. "Good-bye, Daddy! Dear old Dad!"

"Y'bum!"

(12)

It was smooth sailing after a while. I had the old Dorbzeldge eating out of the palm of my hand. Even Fafner admitted that I was handling the machine okay.

"So what's your plan when we get to the Big City?" he asked me.

"Well, I haven't got a plan as such. We'll have to see when we get there."

"What if we see that the people who live there are monsters of some kind, and eat people—or even worse, dogs?"

"Oh, I don't think that will happen."

"Why not?"

"Well, because nothing dangerous has happened so far."

"Your uncle got gleeped," Fafner said. "We were stuck a million miles from noplace with a Bloboform. You nearly drove us over the edge in the parking lot. We're traveling through time-space-and-the-other—and neither of us knows what those are really. The road is a sort of ribbon of light, on both sides of which is endless blackness, and if you had a flat tire, or needed to sneeze at the wrong moment, we'd probably drift away and die. Between us we've got nothing but a bag of kibble—which actually belongs to me, by the way, and I'm just sharing it with you temporarily. We're heading for some Big City we were told about by a shapeless idiot who's never been there, and isn't even sure it exists—and you say nothing dangerous has happened so far! If you ask me we're doomed. We're as good as dead right now. We *are* dead, only we don't know it."

"Now, look," I said. "I was hoping I wouldn't have to speak to you this way, but you force me. I am a human being, whereas you are only a dog—a lower animal. I have the power of reason, and I have superior judgement. If I tell you everything is all right—it's all right. I give the orders, understand?"

"You know what a schmo is?" Fafner asked.

"Yes."

"Well, you're one."

The truth is, I wasn't all that confident. I just thought it would be better not to let Fafner get depressed. He remained quiet in the backseat, not saying a word.

We'd been zooming along for a number of hours. Everything was going smoothly. I was sort of enjoying driving the Dorbzeldge, and that made me feel sad—I missed Borgel. I thought how this would be fun if he were with us. Fafner was continuing to give me the silent treatment.

The road had been a continuous and uninterrupted ribbon of light. All around us was blackness—with the occasional distant glow of a star or something. At times, it was hard to know whether I was asleep or awake. I wished Fafner would say something to break the monotony.

Finally he spoke. "Pick that guy up!"

In the distance, I could just make out a figure standing at the side of the road.

"A hitchhiker?"

"Pick him up! Pick him up!"

"Listen, Fafner. It isn't a good idea to pick up hitchhikers. Don't you know that?"

"Pick him up! Pick him up!" Fafner was shrieking.

"No kidding. It's dangerous. Especially way out here. I mean, he could be a robber or a murderer. We'd better not."

"Pick him up! Pick him up! It's Borgel, you idiot!"

I stepped on the brakes.

Uncle Borgel got into the car. "Hoo boy! That was some experience! Did you guys have fun while I was gone?"

(13)

"Master, never leave me alone with this idiot again," Fafner said.

"Hey! No fair! I took good care of him," I said.

"Look who's driving! You're doing a good job, Melvin. Where were you heading?"

"We were on our way to the Big City."

"Poifect! That's just where I wanted to go," Borgel said.

"I smell a skunk," Fafner said.

(14)

"Yep. I found a good one," Borgel said.

"Say, I have a good idea," I said. "Let's throw the skunk out."

"Are you kidding? We can make a fortune with this carcass," Uncle Borgel said, pulling the flat skunk out of a paper bag he was carrying.

"Well, what if we put the skunk in the trunk?" I asked. "Maybe we could sort of wrap it in a plastic bag."

"Yes. Let's do that before I barf," Fafner said.

"Can't find the key," Borgel said.

"As luck would have it, I found it," I said.

"So pull over, princess, if you're too delicate to ride with a squashed skunk in the front seat."

"Hey, take my bag of kibble out of there!" Fafner said. "I don't want it riding with that thing."

"Such sissies," Borgel said.

When we transferred the dead skunk to the trunk, Borgel and I swapped places, and he took over the driving. It was just as well. I was pretty tired. As soon as we were moving, and most of the skunk perfume had cleared out of the Dorbzeldge's interior, I fell fast asleep.

I woke up in broad daylight. I was stretched out on the

seat with my coat over me. Uncle Borgel must have put it there. I could hear Borgel outside making a great deal of noise, singing and banging and rattling what sounded like pots and pans. It hadn't quite dawned on me that the Dorbzeldge wasn't moving, and Borgel's voice coming from the vicinity of the rear bumper didn't make a whole lot of sense.

When I sat up, I saw trees and bushes and the smoke of a half-dozen campfires. Looking around through the windows of the Dorbzeldge, I saw that we were in as strange a place as I'd ever seen. It looked like a dump. There were piles of old junk, rusted car bodies, piles of old plywood, dead buses and trucks, and other things that might have been spaceships. There were stovepipes sticking out of the piles of junk—and smoke was coming out of some of them. I saw people, and things like people, sitting around on folding chairs and on boxes. Some of the beings were doing the wash, chopping wood, talking, cooking over campfires, and engaging in all sorts of activities. It was like a town made out of garbage.

It had been a long time since I was in a place with things like ground, sky, trees, and light. Later I found out that only the Interstate was like that. Where you were someplace, it tended to be a place similar to Earth, more or less.

I climbed out of the Dorbzeldge. Borgel had the trunk open and was cooking in an improvised kitchen—a folding table with a little gas stove on it beneath a hunk of cloth attached to the open trunk lid at one end and to a mop handle poked into the ground at the other. Borgel was stirring something in a frying pan, and Fafner was sitting nearby watching and drooling.

"I hope you're hungry," he said. "I'm making something special—cornmeal mush with Mexican peppers. It's my favorite camping-out breakfast."

"What is this place? And where did you get the food?" I asked. The cornmeal mush with Mexican peppers looked lethal—but it wasn't dog kibble.

"This is the famous Gypsy Bill's Resort and Spa and Hobo Camp and Junkyard," Uncle Borgel said. "As to the food, I made a deal with the proprietor for a part interest in our skunk. I told you it would come in handy.

"I've been here before. Of course, the place isn't what it was. In my day all sorts of really distinguished people used to stay here. Now, Gypsy Bill Junior—he's the son of the founder—appears to let just anybody in. Also, he's added a duck farm since the last time I was here. Smell that?"

I could smell it. Uncle Borgel directed me to the wash house, which was just behind a clump of bushes, and told me to hurry back. "Breakfast will be served in five minutes on the front fender," he said.

The wash house was an old shack, ready to fall down. When I got back to the Dorbzeldge, Uncle Borgel had arranged breakfast on the fender and hood. In addition to his special favorite camping-out breakfast, there was also some goat cheese from Gypsy Bill Junior's goat, reconstituted mango juice, figs, and raw peanuts. Ordinarily, I might have had some criticisms about the food, but after living on licorice root beer floats and dog food, it was heaven. I had a little of everything, and Fafner made a pig of himself.

While we were eating, Gypsy Bill Jr. himself came by. He was tall and fat with a clip-on earring on one ear, and he wore two hats, one on top of the other.

"Ah, my guests," Gypsy Bill Jr. said. "Is everything to your satisfaction?"

"Everything is first-rate, Bill Jr.," Borgel said. "It does my heart good to see how you've kept the place up since the old days."

"Then you were the guest of my dear late father, Bill Senior?"

"Oh yes," Borgel said. "I used to spend whole summers here."

"I wish you had given me some advance notice that you were coming," Gypsy Bill Jr. said. "I could have cleared the chickens out of the Presidential Suite."

"That would have been nice," Borgel said. "Perhaps we'll come this way again."

"If you do, make sure to wire ahead. Then you won't have to sleep in your car. We can have the Presidential Suite hosed out and freshened up on a day's notice. Is that cornmeal mush with Mexican peppers you're eating?"

"My speciality," Borgel said. "Would you care for some? There's more than enough."

"Thank you," Bill Jr. said. "Running a first-class resort and duck farm gives me an appetite like an ox."

Gypsy Bill Jr. spoke the truth. He not only ate as much

as an ox might have eaten, he also made the same sort of noises.

"If you like, I'll be pleased to read your fortunes in the tea leaves," Gypsy Bill Jr. said. "No charge, of course, just a free reading for my guests."

"So you are carrying on the psychic work of your esteemed father," Borgel said. "I, for one, would be very interested to have you read our fortunes—especially for free. The tea leaves are wild blueberry and mint—will that make a difference?"

"Not in the slightest, my dear sir," Gypsy Bill Jr. said. "Just pour what's left of the tea in my hat." Bill Jr. removed the uppermost of his hats and held it out, upside down. Borgel dumped the contents of his portable aluminum kettle into the hat.

"We'll just shake it up to get the wet out," Gypsy Bill Jr. said, and flipped his hat up and down. All the time, cold blueberry-and-mint tea was dripping through the crown of the hat and onto Gypsy Bill Jr.'s shoes.

"Okay. That's about right. Now to read 'em," he said.

"Watch this," Borgel whispered. "I've seen his father do this. If he's half as good, it will be a treat."

Gypsy Bill Jr. gave a shrill hoot and leaped three or four feet straight into the air. Continuing to hoot, he rolled around on the ground, thrashing and kicking his feet. All this time, he was twisting and pounding on the hat full of soggy tea leaves. Then he sat up and began bouncing around on his bottom, covering a good bit of territory. He struggled to his feet, staggered as if he were hurt, clutching the dripping hat to his stomach, and then began to hop up and down until he was exhausted. Then he collapsed on the ground, panting. He was drenched with sweat and tea. Gypsy Bill Jr. lay on the ground for some time, getting his breath back. Finally, he sat up, pulled the hat open, and looked inside.

"Hooo boy!" he shouted. "You fellows have got *some* fortune!"

(15)

It turned out that Gypsy Bill Jr. charged nothing to read a fortune, but if you wanted to find out what he had read, it would cost you twenty dollars. Uncle Borgel turned down the offer.

"I'm sorry," he said. "It's a matter of principle with me. I never pay to have my fortune told."

Gypsy Bill Jr. walked away dripping and mumbling. Uncle Borgel whispered, "Confidentially, I'd have paid him twenty dollars *not* to tell us our fortunes."

"Can he really do it?" Fafner asked.

"I suppose so. His father could do it every time."

"If you think he's really able to tell what's going to happen, wouldn't it be useful to know in advance?" I asked.

"It would be a great big bore to know in advance," Uncle Borgel said. "I know what I'm talking about. If you know what's going to happen in advance, there would be no surprises—hence, no fun."

"Speaking of what's going to happen," I said, "are we going to keep traveling, or have we settled down at Gypsy Bill's Resort and Spa and Junkyard and Duck Farm?"

"Good point," Uncle Borgel said. "We've had our

breakfast, and we've had our fortunes read but not told. Now, let's get packed up and on the road before this beautiful day is wasted. Where'd the dog go?"

I put two fingers in my mouth and whistled the way Borgel did. Fafner appeared from behind the Presidential Suite and bounded into the car. Borgel was busy packing up the portable kitchen, when Gypsy Bill Jr. appeared again. This time he was leading his goat.

"You wouldn't be headed out Bugleville way, would you?" Bill Jr. asked.

"Might be," Borgel said.

"You wouldn't mind taking a rider along?" Gypsy Bill asked. "I know someone who might be going in that direction."

"It isn't the goat, is it?" Borgel asked.

"No, it's a human, far as I can tell."

"In that case, sure," Uncle Borgel said. "I wouldn't mind taking the goat, but we've got a dog with us, and they might get to fighting."

"That's really nice of you," Gypsy Bill Jr. said. "How about ten dollars and I'll only tell your futures through next Thursday?"

"No deal," Borgel said.

"Well, no hard feelings," Bill Jr. said. "By the way, I never did catch your name. What is it?"

"General Venustiano Carranza," Borgel said.

"Of course," Gypsy Bill Jr. said. "I didn't recognize you without your whiskers. I'll go and get your passenger."

"Hurry it up," Borgel said. "We're leaving in five minutes."

Then he said to me as Gypsy Bill Jr. went to get our rider, "Never give your right name on the road."

(16)

The passenger Gypsy Bill Jr. brought us was a man even shorter than Uncle Borgel. His head was bald and he had a bushy white beard that reached past his knees, which is to say almost to the ground. He wore a sort of shirt that came all the way down to the tops of his boots, which were big yellow ones with thick soles. He had a knapsack and a sign. The sign was a piece of cardboard with the word KA-POP? painted on it.

This was the conversation that passed between Borgel and our passenger:

"Nov shmoz ka-pop?" the little man asked.

"Kopka posto Bugleville," Borgel said.

"Ka-pop?" the little man repeated.

"Popso nokka," Borgel said.

"Pop-ka shmoz nov-ka. Nov shmoz ka-pop?" said the little man.

"Popoosco nobba ka-poppock," Borgel said.

"Hee hee hee!" said the little fellow. He jumped up and down, evidently very happy.

The bearded guy clambered into the backseat of the Dorbzeldge. Fafner appeared to like him. At least, he didn't snarl.

"What were you talking about with him?" I whispered to Borgel.

"I have no idea," Borgel whispered back. "I was just trying to be polite. I have a gift for languages, but I never know what they mean. I think he was talking French."

"That's not French," I said.

"You may be right," Borgel said. "Anyway, he seems like a nice fellow. Maybe he'll tell an amusing story on the way."

Borgel was right. At least the strange man chattered away from the moment the Dorbzeldge started rolling. He was evidently convinced that Borgel could understand what he was saying. Borgel encouraged him in this belief by answering him in his own strange language.

"Ka-poski nopsi hada-dada ka-poosh?" the stranger said as we pulled out of Gypsy Bill's Resort and Spa and Junkyard and Duck Farm, waving to Gypsy Bill Jr. and his goat.

"Poopsi nopsi ka-bash ka-bash nootzle?" Borgel said.

It must have been just the right thing, because the stranger immediately answered, "Oooh, nopsi voot ka-bash sooboo fooey!"

Borgel nodded his head and said, "Difko. Fooey na-voot!"

At this point, the stranger laughed quite a bit, shaking his head and repeating, "Voot-na, voot-na, voot-na! He ha ha ha!"

"Do you have any idea what you two are talking about?" I asked Borgel.

"I believe I'm starting to pick up the language," Borgel

said. "I honestly don't know how I do it. As far as I can tell, this man used to be either the advisor of a great king, or millionaire or president—something like that—or possibly a tailor, a bookie, or a kosher butcher. In any case, he's out of a job now. Also, he's interested in stopping at any zoos we may happen to pass. He's never seen a penguin and it's bothering him."

"You were able to understand all that?"

"I'm not sure, of course," Borgel said. "He may also have been telling us that he has a very contagious disease. I'll try to talk with him some more."

"Pa-poosh chazza inbud nofski?" he said to the little man.

"Kla-bash ta voot-ka hada-dada ka-pop," the little man said. Then he said, "Also, if you see one of those root beer places, please stop. I'd like to buy you all a drink."

"You speak English!" I shouted.

"So do you!" the little man shouted back.

"You never said you spoke English," I said.

"How do you know?" the bearded fellow said.

"So how did I do, speaking your language?" Borgel asked.

"Not bad," the little man said. "You said you were a politically corrupt sardine and you wanted to eat the tires off motorcycles."

"Really? I said that?"

"Like a native."

"I don't know how I do it," Borgel said.

"So how about stopping for a root beer?" the little man said.

"No!" Fafner and I shouted.

"I could use one," Borgel said. "We'll be on the lookout for one of those places with the orange signs."

"Please! Not root beer!" I begged.

"Those are the ones," the stranger said. "They serve it in a frosted mug."

"Yummy!" Borgel said.

"Oh God, no," Fafner said.

"So who are you anyway?" Borgel asked our little passenger.

(17)

"I am Pak Nfbnm*," the little man said.

"*?"

"Exactly."

"I'm pleased to make your acquaintance," Borgel said. "I am Doctor Wiley Sinclair. This is my great-grand nephew, Colonel Sebastian Moran—and our dog, Shep."

Fafner and I nodded formally to Pak Nfbnm*.

"I am deeply honored," Pak Nfbnm* said.

"No more so than ourselves," Borgel said. "You appear to be a person of distinction. If you have no objection, might I ask the nature of your journey?"

"Certainly," Pak Nfbnm* replied. "For the most part, I travel for pleasure, and to gain knowledge of the various times and places I encounter. I also enjoy sending postcards and souvenirs of my travels to my friends and relations at home. I am a native of Benton Harbor, Michigan, where my family has been engaged in the tapioca industry for many generations."

"Who has not heard of Nfbnm*'s Tapioca?" Borgel said. "And you say you travel for pleasure? How long have you been away from home?"

"This time, something over eighty years," Pak Nfbnm*

said. "I'm a habitual traveler in time-space-and-the-other. You might say I'm sort of a professional tourist."

"The same as myself!" Borgel shouted.

"I knew it!" Pak Nfbnm* said. "I could tell at once that I had fallen in with a good crowd! Let's be friends! You may call me Freddie."

"With pleasure!" Borgel said.

"And I will call you Borgel, Melvin, and Fafner. I believe those are the names by which you address one another. We may as well abandon formality, since we're all adventurers together."

"Put 'er there, Freddie," Borgel said, reaching over the seat back and shaking hands with the little time tourist.

"Were you on your way anywhere in particular?" Freddie asked.

"We were considering heading for the Big City," Borgel said. His voice became confidential. "I am the principal stockholder in a fine squashed skunk, and I thought I might as well take it where I can get the highest price."

"Congratulations," Freddie said. "But if I might venture a word of advice, the squashed skunk market is depressed at the moment. You might do well to wait a while, and sell your skunk at the great fair and market which begins in a couple of weeks. Meanwhile, if I might make a further suggestion, could you be persuaded to consider taking a little detour?"

"I can always be persuaded to take a little detour," Borgel said. "What did you have in mind?"

"Have you any particular interest in popsicles?"

"I can't say that I have," Borgel said.

"I have," Fafner said.

"Well, I have always been strongly interested in popsicles of all sorts," Freddie said. "I'm not referring only to the well-known trademark 'Popsicle,' manufactured by the Popsicle Company, a firm almost as old and well-respected as Nfbnm*'s Tapioca, but to the generic popsicle, meaning any sort of frozen water-based confection on a stick—an ice-pop, in other words, or a quiescently frozen dessert stick, also Italian Ices, Fudgsicles, and ice cubes with toothpicks in them, made of everything from raspberry soda to chicken soup."

"Fascinating," Fafner said.

"Probably, my personal all-time favorite is the root beer popsicle," Freddie said.

"Yich. Yich," Fafner and I said.

"So you like popsicles. What about it?" Borgel asked.

"When you like popsicles as much as I do, it's natural to be interested in them," Freddie said. "It shouldn't surprise you that I've traveled millions of miles and thousands of light years in pursuit of rare and exotic popsicles."

"Doesn't surprise me a bit," Fafner said. This was almost the first time I'd ever seen Fafner take much interest in what anyone was saying.

"I don't wish to brag, but it's a certainty that I have tasted more different varieties of popsicles and their cognates than any being who is alive or ever was alive. What is more, I have the honor of being a Commander of the Ancient Order of Popsicle Lovers, and five years ago received a special gold medal for my many contributions to the field. I have it here." Freddie showed us a gold medal in the shape of a popsicle.

"I am also the author of a book, *Popsikellen, Geist und Wissenschaft,* which I wrote in German to show that it was really serious. It runs more than nine hundred pages and is considered the last word on the subject."

"Wow," I said. I felt that I ought to say something.

"And, of course, there have been my many contributions to scholarly journals dealing with popsicles, and frozen desserts, in general, and my humble contribution to the artistic side of the field—the banana popsicle."

"You invented that?" Fafner said with real admiration.

"Someone else would have if I hadn't," Freddie said modestly. "It's always like that when an idea's time has come."

"So what you're telling us," Borgel said, "is that you are the greatest expert alive on the subject of popsicles."

"In a word, yes," Freddie said.

"And why are you telling us this?" Borgel asked.

"Well, first of all to show off," Freddie said. "But also to prepare you for what I am about to tell you. What would you say if I told you there was one ultimate popsicle, a popsicle above all others, a sort of supreme popsicle, beside which all other popsicles melt into nothingness?"

(18)

"I'd be thunderstruck," Borgel said.

"I'd want to know where to find one," Fafner said.

"Not one—it," Freddie said. "There is only one. It is not a type or kind of popsicle, but the ideal of all popsicles."

"I don't get it," I said. "If this popsicle is so good, why is there only one? Why don't they make a lot of them?"

"You don't get it," Freddie said. "The popsicle of which I speak was not 'made' by anyone—at least not in the sense you understand. This popsicle is probably ancient—it may have existed before humans, or any intelligent form of life as we know it. It isn't something you would buy at the corner store and slurp on your way home. It is the essence of popsicle—the beginning of all popsicles. It is the Great Popsicle."

"Amazing," Fafner said.

"This Great Popsicle has powers of which we know nothing. It may have consciousness—I don't know. It may be alive."

"A living popsicle?"

"It's possible. All anyone knows about it is gathered from old stories, forgotten by nearly everyone. I first heard of it long ago while traveling in a mountainous region on a distant world. The people there had had no contact with anyone from outside for centuries before I came. They told stories of a Great Popsicle which contained the essence of all wisdom. I wondered if there might be any truth to the stories. Years later, I found references to a mighty popsicle in a collection of Paleo-Siberian folktales. The obscure Blechkut people, almost extinct, told of a popsicle similar to the one described by those remote mountain people. Then I really began to wonder if such a popsicle might exist."

"Wait!" Borgel shouted. "I know a story about a Great Popsicle. They used to tell it in the Old Country when somebody died."

"Can you remember it?" Freddie asked, very excited.

"Well, let me see," Borgel said. "It went something like this. In the long ago time, when everything was green, people were happy and overweight. There were plenty of skunks, and the crops were abundant. In those days, people did not know how to build houses—and they had no need of them. They would lie down in the fields and go to sleep, and in the morning they would get up and dance.

"At this time there was a king, Napnik. He had a beautiful golden beard and was able to throw a rock farther than any of his subjects. The people loved Napnik because he never bothered them. He lived as simply as his people, except that he had a little cart, drawn by six peasants, in which he would ride around, displaying his beard to everyone's delight.

"Once a year, Napnik would assemble the oldest and wisest men in the land, and they would discuss how to deal with any problems that existed. Since there never were any problems, they would just sit around for a couple of days sucking on potatoes and saying poetry. Then the wise old men would return to their fields and forests for another year.

"It went on like this, as it had in Napnik's father's time, and his father's before him, and his father's before that, and his father's before that, and his father's before that, and his father's before that, and his father's before that, and his father's before that, and his father's . . .'"

"Get on with it!" Freddie shouted.

"Sorry," Borgel said. "That's just the way they'd tell the story in the Old Country."

"They had plenty of time, eh?" Freddie said.

"Nothing but. Anyway . . . his father's before him, etcetera, etcetera. It so happened that Napnik had a daughter, Glossolalia, a great beauty. She also had a golden beard, but not as thick as Napnik's. Glossolalia was not only beautiful, but clever. She tended her father's skunks and could throw a rock as far as the strongest man.

"One year, when the old wise men had gathered to suck on potatoes, Napnik announced, 'It is time for Glossolalia, my beautiful daughter, to marry. How shall we select a suitable husband for her?'

"The old wise men debated and deliberated. More potatoes were sent for. Napnik the King listened patiently as the old wise men discussed the qualities necessary in a husband for the daughter of the king. Two weeks went by, and finally the council of the wise old men had decided. The husband of Glossolalia should be a nice fellow, have a few skunks of his own, be good at throwing rocks, and if possible should have a golden beard and plenty of muscles.

"Napnik was well pleased by the decision of the old wise men, and was about to send them on their way, laden with gifts of skunks and extra potatoes, when something extraordinary occurred. Glossolalia herself strode into the circle of wise men.

"This was something that had never happened before. In those days, although women were feared as they are today, they never appeared in the council of the wise. Even more unthinkable, Glossolalia actually spoke.

" 'Phooey!' she said. 'A nice fellow with skunks? This is the sort of husband you choose for me? I reject your suggestion. I will choose my own husband. Call together all the young men of the country, and I will speak to them myself.'

"With that, Glossolalia kicked potato skins at the old wise men and departed. Napnik and the old wise men were astounded, but the king was moved to action. First, he took back the presents he had given the old wise men, and bade them go. To hurry them on their way, he threw rocks after them.

"Then he called all the young men of the country together. There were eleven of them. Glossolalia came before them, and spoke to them. 'It is time for me to choose a husband,' she said. 'Him that I marry will be king one day, for my father has no other child than me. You are all worthy young men, with skunks and everything, so how shall I choose? This is how. Are you listening? I will marry only a man of courage and wit. Those of you who hope to gain my hand will go far from this country, beyond the great forest, and learn the secrets of the world, do various brave things, and bring me a present. I get to keep the present, whether I marry you or not. The one of you who goes to the most interesting places, and does the bravest things, and brings the best present, gets me. What do you say?"

"While Glossolalia spoke, ten of the eleven young men left. Only one remained, Grebitz, a handsome young skunkherd. Grebitz spoke: 'Glossolalia, Princess, Beauteous One—the other young men have left. I am the only suitor you've got. I am the only one willing to go far from this country and do the other things you said. So why not just get married and save a lot of trouble?'

" 'Not so fast, handsome youth,' Glossolalia said. 'How do you know those other swains didn't leave early just to get started on their travels to win my hand?'

" 'Because there they are, most of them, over in the next field tending the skunks,' Grebitz said.

"Glossolalia picked up a rock. 'Get started, my beloved, before I bean you,' she said.

"Grebitz left on his great journey, the first person in history to leave the Old Country. While he was gone, Glossolalia got tired of waiting, and married someone else."

"Not only is that the most boring story I ever heard," Freddie said, "but it has nothing to do with popsicles."

"That was just to get you in the mood," Borgel said. "The popsicle part comes in the story that goes with it, 'The Travels of Young Grebitz.'"

Fafner was sleeping. I was looking out the window.

"Well, get to it before I die of old age," Freddie said.

(19)

"Okay, 'The Travels of Young Grebitz.' Here goes," Borgel said.

"Wait! Wait! Stop!" Freddie shouted.

"You don't want to hear it?"

Freddie was very excited. "Stop! Stop the car! Back up! I think I saw it!"

"What did you see?" Borgel asked.

"Back up! Back up slowly! It's right in here somewhere," Freddie said. He was leaning out the window.

"What did he see?" Borgel asked me.

"I don't know," I said. "I wasn't paying attention."

"Come on, back up more," Freddie said, motioning with his hand. "A little more. More. Stop! There! There it is!"

We looked where Freddie was pointing. All we saw was a narrow path, somewhat overgrown with weeds, leading back to a sort of hole in the bushes that lined the road. There was a faded sign painted on a piece of wood: GREAT POPSICLE MONUMENT AND PARK.

"Is that it?" I asked.

"Well, read for yourself," Freddie said.

"What are we waiting for? Let's go in," Fafner said.

Borgel headed the Dorbzeldge onto the path, which was bumpy, and we drove into the bushes.

"It looks as though no one has come this way for some time," Borgel said.

The path took us into a dark forest. Branches brushed the sides of the Dorbzeldge.

"Did you know this park existed?" Borgel asked Freddie.

"Not exactly," Freddie said. "I had reason to believe the Great Popsicle might be found somewhere around here, but I never dreamed it would be this easy."

"The sign said Great Popsicle Monument and Park," Borgel said. "It doesn't necessarily mean the Popsicle itself is here."

"Of course it's here!" Freddie said. "What else would be in a place called Great Popsicle Monument and Park?"

"We'll see when we get there—if we ever get there," Borgel said. "This path seems to go on forever."

Of course the path didn't go on forever—just for about an hour. After a while, we all were wondering if we hadn't somehow missed the Great Popsicle Monument and Park.

"How big is this Great Popsicle?" Borgel asked.

"I'm not sure," Freddie said. "It has to be pretty big. I mean, it's a great popsicle, not some dinky little thing. I don't see how we could miss it."

"I think I see something!" Fafner said.

There was something barely showing through the trees a long way ahead of us. As we got closer, we could see it was a large wooden building in a clearing. The building was a sort of round barn, like a fat tower or a silo. It needed a coat of paint. There was nothing in the area around the building but an old car. It looked abandoned. The door of the building was open. Over the door was a sign: GREAT POPSICLE.

"This is it! This is it!" Freddie shouted. "Come on, everybody! Let's go in."

"Hold it!" a voice called from somewhere. We looked around. Then we saw a skinny, dirty-looking man emerge from the old car. The way he was stretching suggested that he'd been sleeping in it.

"You folks gonna go in and see the Popsicle?" the skinny guy asked.

"Yes. It's all right, isn't it?" Freddie asked.

"Cost you fifty zlotys a head," the skinny guy said.

"Fair enough," Freddie said, paying him. "It's my treat. You are all my guests at this historic moment."

We thanked Freddie and followed him into the building. He was hopping with excitement.

Immediately inside the door was a set of dusty wooden steps. We went up, through a hot, narrow corridor. It was just like going up to the loft of an old barn. The stairs wiggled and creaked under our feet.

When we came out of the stairway, we were standing on a sort of balcony that went all around the inside of the round building. The whole interior was one open space— just like a barn. Light came from a few windows above our heads. We could look down from the balcony to the floor, which was dirt. In the middle of the floor, standing about fifteen feet high, the top of it a little higher than our heads, the sides of it just beyond the reach of our hands, was a huge, vast, outsized Popsicle.

It was the old-fashioned double kind—two sticks. It was orange. It was dusty on the top.

"That's it?" I asked.

"The Great Popsicle," Freddie said rapturously.

Fafner's nose was twitching a mile a minute. "I don't think so," he said.

"What do you mean, you don't think so?" Freddie asked.

"I don't think it's the Great Popsicle," Fafner said.

"I thought I explained to you," Freddie said. "I am the greatest expert in the universe on the subject of popsicles. While I am not yet a hundred-percent satisfied that this is indeed the Great Popsicle, I can't see any way it could be anything else. Now I ask you, what makes you think it's not?"

"I'm a dog, bozo," Fafner said. "I can sniff circles around a humanoid like you. If my olfactory membrane were spread out it would take up more area than my whole skin. I can find out more by sniffing for a second that you could find out in a library in a year."

"And your sniffer tells you this isn't the Great Popsicle?"

"That's what my sniffer tells me."

"You know what the Great Popsicle should smell like?"

"I know it shouldn't smell like papier-mâché and epoxy and wood and chicken wire."

"That's what this thing is made of?" I asked.

"Plus, it isn't cold. If it were a popsicle, it would have to be frozen—that's basic, isn't it, Freddie?"

"Yes."

"Well, do any of you feel any cold coming from that thing? It's hotter in here than outside. I rest my case. It's a fake."

"Well, I was coming to that conclusion myself," Freddie said. "Just the emotion of the moment—the illusion of seeing it—confused me. Fafner here—intuitive, simple beast that he is—may have gotten straight to the truth of the matter without doing any actual thinking."

Fafner made a noise I'd have thought could only be made by an animal with lips.

"Still," Borgel said, "what's the purpose of this big statue? What's it doing here, and what does it mean? We are certainly in Great Popsicle country, even if this isn't the genuine article. There's plenty to find out."

"Indeed," Freddie said. "I suggest we question the yokel who took my money on the way in."

We hurried down the stairs and found the yokel.

"You came out in a hurry," the skinny guy said. "Didn't you like what it had to say?"

"I'd like to ask you a few questions, if you please, my good man," Freddie said.

"I'm not a good man. I'm a bad man. And I don't get paid for answering questions. I get paid for selling tickets to the Popsicle," the skinny guy said.

Uncle Borgel put his hand on the skinny guy's shoulder. "Of course, my colleague would compensate you for your time."

"My time is pretty expensive," the skinny guy said. "How about two hundred zlotys for as long as it takes to give us a little information?"

"Okay," said the skinny guy. "Let's have the money, and then ask your questions."

Freddie handed over the zlotys. "First of all, can you tell us what that thing in there is supposed to be?"

"That's the Popsicle. That all you want to know?"

"It isn't a real popsicle—"

"That a question?"

"—is it?"

"Nope. It's what you call a replica."

"All right, now we're getting somewhere, however slowly," Freddie said. "What is it a replica of?"

"Boy, this is fun," the skinny guy said. "If I had known how easy answering questions was, I would have done it before this. It is a replica of a popsicle."

"Any particular popsicle?"

"Maybe. I don't know the answer to that one. You'd have to ask the guy who made it."

"That was going to be my next question. Who made it?"

"My daddy."

"Your daddy?"

"Yep. Daddy built it."

"Is Daddy anywhere around?"

"Yep, he's right over near the house. But he won't answer any of your questions, if that's what you're thinking."

"Not even for two hundred zlotys?"

"Not for two million. Daddy's been dead for twenty years. He's buried near the house."

"Well then, who *was* your late father?"

"Evil Toad."

"I beg your pardon?"

"Evil Toad. It's a family name."

"I see."

"I am Hapless Toad. We Toads have lived here, oh, forever."

"Look, why did your father, Evil Toad, build that popsicle?"

"Why ask me?"

"Why ask you? Who else is there to ask?"

"Well, I don't mean to be rude, but why come all the way back here, and pay fifty zlotys each, for you three gentlemen and the dog, and go in to see the Popsicle and not ask any questions?"

"But I am asking questions, you rural Toad!"

"Yes, but you're asking *me*!"

Freddie was hopping up and down now. "Who else is there to ask?"

"Why, the Popsicle. Didn't you know it answers questions?"

"It answers questions?"

"And you think I'm a yokel. Yes, it does. Why would anyone drive way back here in the woods and pay fifty zlotys just to look at some statue of a popsicle? My goodness, you're ignorant."

"The *Popsicle* answers questions?"

"I just told you. I was wondering why you all came

out of there so fast. When Rolzup, the Martian High Commissioner, was here the other month he stayed in there most of the day."

"Rolzup came here?"

"Lots of people come here."

"Who's Rolzup?" I whispered to Bogel.

"A very important person. Some people say he's the only person in the universe who knows what's going on," Borgel whispered back.

"So what do you do, just ask it questions?"

"That's right."

"And it answers?"

"Some. It answers some."

"Questions about anything?"

"You can ask about anything, I guess. It answers what it likes."

"So there really isn't much point asking you."

"Not much."

"When we could just go back in and ask the Popsicle."

"So it would seem."

"Well, Hapless Toad, thank you very much for explaining everything."

"You're welcome, I'm sure."

"We'll just go back inside now."

"Do what you like."

"Let's go back inside," Freddie said.

We started toward the door.

"Hold it!" Hapless Toad called. "That will cost you fifty zlotys a head."

"We already paid!"

"Then you came out. It costs fifty zlotys to go in."

"But we didn't ask any questions."

"That makes no difference. Fifty zlotys to go in."

"That's robbery!"

"Rules are rules. Pay up."

Freddie counted out two hundred zlotys. "Every place I've ever been, dogs get in free," he said.

"Not here," Hapless Toad said. "Enjoy yourselves. Stay as long as you like."

We made our way up the stairs to the balcony inside the wooden building. There was the replica of the Great Popsicle, just as boring as before.

"How do you propose we go about this?" Borgel asked Freddie.

"Well, I suppose I'll just ask it a question. Great Popsicle, can you hear me?"

From somewhere within the Popsicle, a metallic voice spoke, "Yep. I hear you. Got a question?"

"This is hokey," Fafner growled.

"Try to be scientific," Freddie said. "I'll ask it something simple. Great Popsicle, how much is four times four?"

"Just a minute," the Great Popsicle replica said. We could hear it mumbling to itself. "Let's see . . . fifteen? No, sixteen! Sixteen is the answer."

"The thing is stupid," Fafner said.

"Think it'll rain today?" Freddie asked.

"Nope. Not a cloud in the sky. Had some rain last week though."

Borgel motioned for us to gather close around. He

whispered, "Does that voice sound familiar to anybody?"

"It sounds like Hapless Toad to me," I whispered back.

"Just what I was thinking," Freddie said. "Obviously there's a microphone and speaker inside the replica and the scoundrel is working a trick on us."

Fafner said, "Let me take care of this. Wait here." Without a sound, he disappeared down the stairs.

"Hey! You guys got any more questions?" the Great Popsicle replica called.

"We're thinking," Borgel said.

A minute later, we heard rapid footsteps on the stairs. Hapless Toad appeared, followed closely by Fafner.

"Hey!" Hapless Toad said. "This dog bit me!"

"Nipped you," Fafner said. "If I'd bitten you, you'd know the difference. I found him sitting in that old car, earphones on his head, talking to a microphone hidden in his hat."

"I was listening to my portable stereo!" Hapless Toad complained. "And I was singing along with the Ugly Bug Band, my favorite group. What's wrong with that?"

"What's wrong with that is, one, the Ugly Bug Band is probably the worst insect country-and-western group in the galaxy; two, you are supposed to be fixing the plumbing, not goofing in your car; and three, you have a horrible singing voice," someone said. Or something said. It wasn't any of us. It was the Great Popsicle.

We looked at each other. Evidently, it was not Hapless Toad doing the talking for it, as we had thought.

"Either that or he's a ventriloquist," Borgel said.

"A vent—what?" Hapless Toad asked.

"A ventriloquist, dummy," the Popsicle said. "Someone who can project his voice and make it seem to come from someplace else. Don't you know anything?"

"Whose voice is that?" Freddie asked Hapless Toad.

"My daddy's."

"You said your daddy was dead."

"He is. When he built this thing, he programmed it to sound like him."

"Programmed it?"

"Yes. It's a computer. What did you think it was, magic? I'm going," Hapless Toad said. "Tell your dog if he bites me again I'm going to whack him with a shovel."

Hapless Toad left.

"So you're a computer?" Borgel asked the replica.

"Yes. You want me to explain what a computer is?"

"I know what a computer is. Who built you?"

"Evil Toad, a great genius and inventor."

"Why did he build you?"

"Evil Toad built me because his son, Hapless Toad, whom you've met, is a simple-minded goon. Since his only offspring has the mental power of coleslaw, Evil Toad created me to pass on the wisdom he accumulated in his life."

"Any wisdom in particular?" Borgel asked.

"Yes. Any wisdom in particular."

"Why did Evil Toad build you to resemble a great popsicle?"

"Evil Toad built me to resemble the Great Popsicle, out of respect. He respected the Great Popsicle."

"Why did Evil Toad respect the Great Popsicle?"

"The Great Popsicle was Evil Toad's friend and teacher. It taught him all he knew."

"So the Great Popsicle exists!" Freddie shouted.

"Is that a question?"

"Doesn't it?" Freddie added.

"Beyond question," the Popsicle replica said.

"And you say it was Evil Toad's friend and teacher. Does that mean the Popsicle is a living being?"

"Well, I wouldn't say that," the Popsicle replica computer answered. "A popsicle is a popsicle, however great it may be—otherwise it wouldn't be a popsicle, would it? And all popsicles are friendly, otherwise they wouldn't be so beloved by all humankind and others. As to being Evil Toad's teacher, you can learn a lot from a popsicle. You of all people should know that, Freddie Nfbnm*."

"You know who I am?"

"I know most things."

"You had trouble with four times four," Fafner said.

". . . but I'm a little shaky in arithmetic."

"Great Popsicle computer replica, I desire to find the actual, original Great Popsicle. Where is it?" Freddie asked, very excited.

"Ask not!" the Popsicle replica said ominously.

"Why not?"

"Ask not!"

"You won't tell?"

"I'll tell if you ask, but I ask you, ask not!"

"Why do you ask me to ask not?"

"Ask not that either, if you know what's good for you!"

"But I want to know!" Freddie said.

The computer popsicle was silent.

"Don't I?" Freddie added.

"This is the last time I will warn you," the replica said. "Ask not!"

"And now you'll tell us?"

"Yes."

"So tell us!" Freddie shouted. The Popsicle replica said nothing. Then Freddie added, ". . . won't you?"

"Don't blame me for what happens. Leave here. Take a left at the road. Go four metaparasangs. Turn left again at the statue of a blue-and-orange-striped cow's head. Then you're on a winding road. You go, oh, about eleven metaparasangs. You cross an interdimensional bridge. When you cross the bridge you will have left this plane of existence. You'll be in a monochromatic two-dimensional state. Follow the signs for Terre Haute. This will take you to the Interstate. When you get on the Interstate, turn off at the sign for Hell."

"We're going to Hell?"

"You're going beyond it. Take a right at the end of the ramp. You'll be in a three-dimensional state. Go about a metaparasang, past the Gates of Hell, and look for the Blue Moon Rest. It's a good place to have lunch. Ask Milly, the waitress, if her husband, Glugo, has a boat for rent. Then you have to find a wilderness guide. Maybe Glugo will take you himself. Then you're on your own."

"That's it?"

"Except one more thing, I have to tell you."

"What's that?"

"Don't go."

"Will we be in danger?"

"That is all I have to say on this subject."

"I say let's go!" Freddie said. "What do you say? Do you all want to come with me to find the Great Popsicle?"

"Well, never let it be said that I shrank from an adventure," Borgel said. "Melvin, are you up to this expedition?"

"Sure," I said. "If you want to go, I do, too."

"How about you, Fafner?" Borgel asked.

"I say, let's forget it. Ask the Popsicle if there's an amusement park around here."

"So you vote against going?" Borgel said.

"Emphatically," Fafner said.

"Well, it's too bad the vote wasn't unanimous—but of course, as a dog, you don't really have a vote. I just asked you out of politeness. We'll go. Maybe we'll find an amusement park another time."

"I hope sometime, in another life, I get to be a humanoid, and you have to be a dog," Fafner said.

"Unlikely," Borgel said. "Cheer up. I'll buy you a cheeseburger or something at that diner."

"Phooey on you," Fafner said.

"Now let me get this straight," Freddie said. "We leave here. Take a left at the road. Go four metaparasangs. Turn left again at the statue of a blue-and-orange-striped cow's head. Then we're on a winding road. We go, oh, about eleven metaparasangs. We cross an interdimensional bridge. When we cross the bridge we will have left this plane of existence. We'll be in a monochromatic two-dimensional state. Follow the signs for Terre Haute. This will take us to the Interstate. When we get on the Interstate, turn off at the sign for Hell.

"We take a right at the end of the ramp. We'll be in a three-dimensional state. Go about a metaparasang, past the Gates of Hell, and look for the Blue Moon Rest. Ask Milly, the waitress, if her husband, Glugo, has a boat for rent. Then we have to find a wilderness guide. Maybe Glugo will take us himself. Then we're on our own. Right?"

"Right," said the replica Popsicle computer. "But I wish you wouldn't."

(20)

"It's a long way to the far side of Hell," Borgel said. "I suggest we camp somewhere around here, and get a fresh start in the morning."

"Let's go now," Freddie said. "We can drive all night, and take a rest when we get there."

"I vote for starting in the morning," Fafner said. "Even though I'm only a dog and don't have a vote."

"We'll ask Hapless Toad if there's a good place to camp," Borgel said.

We found Hapless Toad painting a new sign. DOGS MUST BE KEPT ON LEASH it said.

"Mr. Toad, do you know of a place we can camp for the night?" Borgel asked.

"Try Toad's Campground, just up the road," Hapless Toad said.

"Any relation?"

"My cousin Witless Toad runs it. Tell him I sent you."

"Thanks," Borgel said. "We're sorry about the dog attacking you. He thought he was doing right."

"He bit a hole right through my pants," Hapless Toad said.

"I'm sure he's sorry," Borgel said. "By the way, any

place around here we can buy some groceries?"

"Yep. Toad's Store. It's near the campground."

"Another relative?"

"Nope. The guy just happens to be named Toad—Nasty Ugly Horrible Little Toad. Not one of our Toads."

We stopped at Toad's Store. It was one of those country places that sells a little of everything. Only in this case the proprietor, Nasty Ugly Horrible Little Toad, had nothing edible to sell, except onions.

"Onions will be fine," Borgel said. "I was just in the mood for a mess of onions, barbequed over an open fire. How about the rest of you?"

"Nobody touches the bag of kibble, understood?" Fafner said.

"Onions sound fine to me," Freddie said.

We bought a whole bag.

Witless Toad's campground was okay. It was not much different from Gypsy Bill's. We found a nice spot under some trees, and Borgel dug a bunch of blankets out of the trunk of the Dorbzeldge.

"Let's see, a couple of us can bunk in the Dorbzeldge," Borgel said. "And we can make a couple of beds on the ground by gathering some soft branches and folding them under the blankets."

"I prefer to sleep in a tree," Freddie said.

"That's interesting," Borgel said. "Do you always sleep in a tree?"

"Whenever I can," Freddie said.

"Suit yourself," Borgel said.

We spent the rest of the afternoon gathering wood for

the fire and setting up Borgel's portable kitchen. Borgel and I peeled and cut up onions, and skewered them on branches. Night come on suddenly, and it got cool. We gathered around the fire, and cooked our onions-on-a-stick. It was sort of neat. I even liked the onions.

Borgel brewed some Norwegian vole-moss tea in his portable kettle, and we all sat around after supper, drinking tea, and enjoying being outside.

"By this time tomorrow, we may have found the Great Popsicle," Freddie said.

"I wonder if it will be anything like the stories," Borgel said.

"That reminds me," Freddie said. "You never told us the story about Grebitz."

"So I didn't," Borgel said. He got up and walked over to the trunk of the Dorbzeldge. After rummaging around for a while, he came back with a banjo. "Can you handle one of these?" he asked Freddie.

"In an emergency, I suppose I can do pretty well with one," Freddie said.

Borgel handed Freddie the banjo. "Well, let's do it right. You get started, and I'll chime in after a while."

Freddie hefted the banjo. "It's a nice one," he said.

"Be careful where you point it," Borgel said. "Start me off with something repetitive in a minor key."

Freddie clawed at the banjo, making a sort of sad, squeaking sound in his nose at the same time. Borgel took a swig of Norwegian vole-moss tea, and leaned back, his eyes closed. Then he began to speak.

"The true story of 'The Travels of Young Grebitz,'"
Borgel said.

"This is the story of Grebitz, a skunkherd of pure heart,
who ventured far to win the hand of Glossolalia, the
daughter of Napnik the King, and of what he saw, and
where he went, and what he learned, and how he came
back, and what he ate, and what he thought, and how
much the skunks missed him when he was gone. Also of
the amazing thing he encountered, so strange he knew not
what it was, and he knew not what to call it, and how
he learned wisdom from the amazing thing and discovered
it's fearsome secret name."

"Was that the Popsicle?" Freddie asked.

"Keep playing," Borgel said. "And don't interrupt."

"Young Grebitz walked, on foot and alone. He left the
pleasant fields he had known all his life. He left the skunks
he had cared for. He left his friends, the other skunkherds
of the country. He carried with him a leathern bottle of
Hot and Spicy Oil, a potato, and his skunkherd's flute.
Nothing else did he carry, for that was all he owned.

"Grebitz entered the Great Forest, a place of terror, for
here skunks would sometimes stray and never be found
again. For many days, Grebitz wandered in the forest,
nibbling his potato, playing his flute, and listening to the
calls of the forest birds. When night came, he would sleep
on the leafy forest floor, and each night a strange dream
would come to him.

"This is the dream young Grebitz would dream each
night while he wandered in the forest: Grebitz would be
on the very peak of a high mountain. Below him he

116

would see fields and forests and rivers and all the things which existed. As Grebitz dreamed this dream, he would feel great excitement and happiness. Then, in his dream, the ghostly figure of a woman of great height, in billowing robes and wearing green basketball shoes, would appear.

" 'Beware!' the woman would cry. 'Only the pure and simple may taste of the Great Wisdom!'

" 'I am pure and simple!' Grebitz would say. Then, in his dream, the ghostly woman would bash Grebitz on the conk with a stick. He would feel a stinging chill, and then awake.

"Grebitz was puzzled as to what this dream might mean. Night after night in the Great Forest, the dream would come to him, and day after day he wandered.

"At last, Grebitz emerged from the forest. No one in his country had ever come so far. At the edge of the forest he met a giant. The giant was large and hairy and dirty, and smelled like a thousand angry skunks. 'Prepare to die!' the giant said to Grebitz.

" 'Why? What did I do?' Grebitz asked the giant.

" 'You didn't do anything. Just prepare to die, that's all.'

"Grebitz saw there was no way to defeat the giant. He tried to run away, but the giant overtook him. 'Now, *really* prepare to die,' the giant said.

" 'Spare my life,' Grebitz said, 'and I will give you what's left of this potato.'

" 'Ha!' the giant said. 'I'll get that anyway, after you're dead.'

" 'Ha yourself,' Grebitz said. 'You may kill me, but you will never learn the secret of this bottle.' Grebitz held up his leathern bottle of Hot and Spicy Oil.

" 'Who cares?' said the giant. 'And how come that bottle is made of leathern and not the usual stuff?'

" 'Go ahead and kill me,' Grebitz said. 'I will die with the satisfaction that you will never know the secret.'

" 'Fine,' said the giant. 'I'll kill you right now, since you're so satisfied.'

" 'Fine by me. Kill away,' Grebitz said.

" 'Fine,' said the giant.

" 'Fine,' said Grebitz.

" 'Probably there isn't any secret to that bottle anyway,' the giant said.

" 'You'll never know, will you?' said Grebitz.

" 'So what's in there anyway? Something magic?' the giant asked.

" 'I thought you were going to kill me,' Grebitz said. 'Get on with it. I haven't got all day.'

" 'I'll kill you when I'm good and ready,' the giant said. 'So what's in the bottle?'

" 'I'm not telling,' said Grebitz.

" 'You don't have to tell me the secret,' the giant said. 'Just what's in it."

" 'It's a magic elixir,' Grebitz said. 'You drink it and it gives you all sorts of powers.'

" 'Boy, are you stupid!' the giant said. 'You gave the whole thing away.'

" 'No I didn't,' said Grebitz.

" 'Yes you did,' said the giant. 'Now I can kill you and drink the elixir. What a dope.'

" 'It won't do you any good,' Grebitz said. " 'I didn't tell you how much to drink. If you don't drink enough it won't do anything.'

" 'I've had breakfasts that were brighter than you,' the giant said. 'Now you've told me everything.'

" 'No I haven't,' Grebitz said.

" 'Oh yes? You told me that it's a magic elixir that will give me all sorts of powers. Then you told me that if I don't drink enough, it won't do anything. Now, given that I am a giant, and about four times your size, I don't suppose it would be too much if I drank the whole thing, would it?'

" 'Well . . .'

" 'Here, give me that,' the giant said. He snatched the leathern bottle of Hot and Spicy Oil from Grebitz and drank it dry in one gulp. Then, naturally, he fell dead on the spot.

" 'That's funny,' Grebitz said. 'It never does that to me.' "

"Is there a popsicle in this story?" Freddie interrupted.

"I'm getting to it," Borgel said.

"Well, my fingers are getting tired, that's all," Freddie said.

"Before Grebitz's amazed eyes, the dead giant changed into the woman in the flowing robes and green basketball shoes from his dream.

" 'You have shown courage in facing the giant,' the woman said.

" 'I didn't know it would kill him,' Grebitz said.

" 'I know,' the mysterious woman said. 'If you had, you would not be a perfect idiot, and therefore would be unworthy to taste of the Great Wisdom.'

"Then she hit Grebitz on the conk with some sort of stick and he fell unconscious.

"When Grebitz awoke, he was in a meadow full of flowers. Birds sang, and the sun warmed him. He felt an inexpressible happiness. Everything was beautiful and serene.

"Then he saw something strange beyond belief. It was a thing like no other thing he had ever seen. Grebitz did not know if it was a creature, or a strange flower, or an apparition. Whatever the thing was, it filled him with wonder and happiness. It was frolicking and gamboling among the flowers—a shining thing, which seemed to be made of colored ice. It had two tiny legs which looked as though they were sticks of wood, and when it came near to Grebitz, he felt a delightful coolness which seemed to come from the thing.

"He did not know why, but he experienced a great feeling of love for the wonderful object.

" 'What can this miracle be called?' Grebitz asked aloud.

"The mysterious woman with the green basketball shoes appeared beside him.

" 'It has many names,' the woman said. 'In the form you now witness, it is known as the Great Popsicle—and few humanoids have ever seen it.' Then she vanished.

"Grebitz wondered at the Great Popsicle for a long

time. Finally, it pranced away and returned no more. Grebitz rose, and said, 'What an incredible experience. I think I'll continue my travels now.' "

"Wait! Is that the end of the story?" Freddie shouted.

"No, there's more," Borgel said. "But that's all there is about the Popsicle."

"I'm going to bed," Freddie said.

"Don't you want to hear the rest of it?" Borgel asked.

"No." Freddie climbed a tree, wrapped his ankles around a branch, and went to sleep, upside down like a bat.

(21)

"Do *you* want to hear the rest of the story?" Borgel asked me.

"Maybe another time," I said. "Interesting how Freddie's sleeping hanging upside down in a tree."

"That's not all that's interesting about him," Borgel said.

"What do you mean?"

"Freddie is not what he seems to be," Borgel said.

"You mean because he sleeps upside down in trees?"

"That, too. But I was thinking about the way he played the banjo."

"I thought he was pretty good," I said.

"There's something about the way he played it," Borgel said. "I don't exactly know what it was. Something I must have forgotten. Well . . . no matter. I'm sure it will come back to me. Meanwhile, are you having a nice adventure, Melvin?"

"Actually, I've never been on an adventure before, so I don't have anything to compare it to. But I guess it's okay."

"Well, we'll see some interesting things tomorrow,"

Borgel said. "Look, Fafner is asleep already. We should turn in and get our rest."

"Uncle Borgel," I said.

"Yetz?"

"I was just wondering . . . I mean . . . well, it's been a long time since we left home."

"There's no such thing as a long time. I thought I explained that to you. Time is neither long nor short. Remember the elliptical bagel with poppy seeds? The correct thing to say would be 'it's been an elliptical time since we left home.' "

"What I meant was, won't they all be worried about us?"

"Why should they be? We're okay, aren't we?"

"Yes, but we've been gone a long . . . I mean, an elliptical time . . . and . . ."

"Oho! Homesick, is it? Actually, they might not even know we're gone."

"Not know?"

"It's relative. While you have the impression that we've been traveling in time-space-and-the-other for quite a while, it may seem like a minute to the folks back home."

"Really?"

"Oh, absotoomley. Of course, it could work the other way. It might seem to them that we've been gone ninety or a hundred years. It's tricky."

"Really."

"Look, if you want to go home, just say the word. I don't want you to have a bad time."

"We can go home anytime we like?"

"I don't see why not," Uncle Borgel said.

I felt a lot better knowing that. "No, I want to go on and keep having an adventure," I said.

"On the other hand, I don't see why either," Borgel said. "But let's get some sleep. Plenty to do in the morning."

In the morning, after a breakfast of leftover onions, we piled into the Dorbzeldge, and were on the road again.

"Where are we exactly?" I asked Borgel.

"What do you mean, where?" he asked. "We're on a country road, in the Dorbzeldge, looking for a statue of a blue-and-orange-striped cow's head."

"I mean, are we on Earth or some other planet? I never quite worked it out."

"You ever see anybody on Earth who looks like Hapless Toad?" Borgel asked.

"You mean the blue ears?"

"Right."

"No, I can't say that I have."

"So we're on some other planet—or some part of Earth we've never heard of—or a separate plane of existence. It's complicated."

"Explain it to me."

"Well, when you travel in time-space-and-the-other, it's hard to tell which one you're traveling in—or whether it's more than one."

"I don't get it," I said.

"Did you ever see a ghost?" Borgel asked.

"No."

"How about someone who seems to appear for a second and then disappear?"

"No."

"How about one of those soft ice-cream stands, Dairy Chill and so forth?"

"Sure. I've seen plenty of those," I said.

"All right. They're the best example anyway," Borgel said. "All those places exist in another plane of existence. They just tend to appear in the one you usually live in."

"What do you mean another plane of existence?" I asked. I was really confused.

"A different world, which is as real as yours and which exists in the same space, but in a slightly different time. You know what is it a tuning fork?"

"Yes."

"Well, it makes sound by vibrating, right? Vibrating is shaking to and fro. If you look at one closely while it's vibrating, you can see the tines of the fork appearing to exist on the 'to' side, and on the 'fro' side. Now what if you could see the 'to' side of each vibration, but not the 'fro' side? What would happen then?"

"Um, it would seem to disappear and reappear really fast?"

"Prezacktly. So what you might think is a ghost, or someone who appears for a second and then disappears, is just someone who vibrates to and fro, only slowly. And a soft ice-cream stand—don't ask me why it's always them—vibrates to and fro very, very slowly."

"I don't understand," I said.

"I do," Fafner said.

"Look!" Freddie said. "There's the blue-and-orange-striped cow's head!"

We turned onto the winding road.

"Next we have to look for an interdimensional bridge," Freddie said.

"This will be interesting," Borgel said. "Now you'll see what it's like to go from one plane of existence to another."

Interesting was hardly the word for it. Terrifying would be a better word. Also stunning. Also insane. After doodling along the road, which twisted and turned like a snake for a number of hours, we came to the bridge.

It looked like an ordinary bridge. It didn't go over a river or anything—just a bridge. One of those metal highway bridges you see all the time. Except when we were about halfway across, we all turned from color to black and white.

So did everything else. Even stranger, everything became flat. Borgel was flat. Fafner was flat. Freddie was flat. What we, and the Dorbzeldge, and everything outside the Dorbzeldge looked like was cartoons. The daily black-and-white cartoons in the newspaper.

"This is weird! What's happening?" I shouted.

"We're in a two-dimensional state," Borgel said. "Don't try to think any deep thoughts, hee hee hee!"

"You look like a cartoon!" I said. "How can you drive in this flatness?"

"Actually, it's easier," Borgel said. "One less dimension to worry about."

"I hate this," I said.

"You're just used to being round," Borgel said. "It makes a nice change, actually."

"I feel like a place mat," Fafner said.

"You want to see something really unusual?" Borgel asked. He pulled over to the side of the road. "Come on, Fafner! Get out and chase me!"

Fafner and Borgel ran around the car. It was exactly like those old black-and-white cartoons they show on the local cable TV station. It was funny. Anyway, *I* thought it was funny.

Freddie was impatient. "Get back in the car!" he said. "We have a long way to go!"

By this time, Borgel and Fafner were out of breath from running and laughing. "Watch this!" Borgel said. He turned sideways quickly and almost disappeared.

"Hey! Look at this one!" Fafner shouted. He crawled under Borgel's feet. "I'm a rug!"

I jumped out of the car. "Look at me! I can fold myself!" And I did it. I bent over double and folded like a piece of paper.

"Very good. Very good," Freddie said. "Now let's go."

"You're certainly in a big hurry," Borgel said, getting back behind the wheel. "You should have more fun. You'll last longer."

"Bear right for Terre Haute!" Freddie shouted, pointing to a sign.

"I see it. I see it," Borgel said. "Now look for signs for the Interstate."

We passed black-and-white cartoon farms with what looked like drawings of houses and barns and animals.

Fafner seemed to enjoy being two-dimensional. "Look out for paper clips, Borgel!" he chortled. "You know, we could get there faster if we put ourselves in an envelope and mailed ourselves special delivery."

"Not funny," I said.

"Aw, go fold yourself," Fafner said.

When we finally got on the Interstate, we popped back into three dimensions, and full color. I guess I had been starting to get used to being flat and monochrome, because it seemed suddenly very crowded in the Dorbzeldge. For a few minutes, I couldn't get used to taking up space, and I kept bumping into things.

The Interstate was the old familiar blackness and void. The road was the same glowing ribbon beneath us. In the distance there were occasional areas which glowed dimly, and once in a while, a distant flash like lightning.

"Ah, the old Interstate," Borgel said. "So restful."

"Uncle Borgel?"

"Yaas?"

"Remember the big energy ball that chased us the other time?"

"Sure."

"I think I see another one," I said.

"Nope. That's not another one of those energy monsters."

"What a relief!"

"It's the same one. I wonder if it's been following us all this while."

This remark of Borgel's depressed me—especially as

the big peach-colored thing was not behind us but diagonally ahead of us and approaching fast.

"It looks like it's going to get us!" I shouted.

"Oh no! I'm too beautiful to die!" Fafner shouted.

"Actually, it looks sort of bad," Uncle Borgel said. "About the only thing I can think of doing is running off the Interstate, which is pretty much always certain death, from what I've been told."

"Can't we turn around and run the other way?" I asked.

"That would involve stopping," Borgel said. "By the time I did that, and got us turned around, it would be a lot closer, and it would overtake us before we built up speed. No, the best thing would be to swing off the Interstate, and hope we'd come around in an arc going the other way. Or, I could try the same thing, swinging around behind the energy ball—but, as I said, the chances of getting back on the road are almost nonexistent. I think we're probably doomed."

"I know what to do!" Freddie said. He had dug what looked like a potato out of his pocket, and was holding it up for us to see.

"Well, if you like," Borgel said. "But we'll barely have time to eat that before it catches us."

"We aren't going to eat it," Freddie said. He seemed to be whispering to the potato thing. Then he casually tossed it out the window. It hovered in the void outside the Dorbzeldge for an instant, and then made a beeline for the glowing energy monster.

Suddenly the energy ball extinguished, like a light being switched off.

"All gone," Freddie said.

"How'd you do that?" I asked.

"Just a handy trick," Freddie said. "Something I picked up on my travels."

"I hope nobody but us saw you do that," Borgel said. "We aren't supposed to destroy things along the Interstate. We could get in serious trouble."

"We were already in serious trouble," Freddie said.

"True," Borgel said. "Do you have any more of those potatoes on you?"

"No, that was my only one," Freddie said.

"Good," Borgel said. "Weapons scare me."

"What did you mean, 'too beautiful to die'?" I asked Fafner.

"Did I say that?" Fafner asked.

"Amazing the conceit of some animals," I said.

(22)

The signs for Hell appeared along the Interstate long before we got to the turnoff. They said things like GO TO HELL! and SEE YOU IN HELL! and STAY AT THE PRINCE OF DARKNESS MOTOR LODGE—BAR-B-QUES NIGHTLY.

Then there was a big sign: HELL, NEXT EXIT.

Borgel turned the Dorbzeldge off the Interstate onto Good Intentions Boulevard. I have to say it. It was fantastic.

Never in my life had I seen so many electric signs, so many fast-food restaurants, motels, shopping malls, drive-in movies, used-car lots, roadside stands, billboards, miniature golf courses, and discount hardware stores.

The traffic was astounding. Vehicles of every imaginable description were progressing at a crawl, in three lanes, bumper to bumper. There were cars and buses, spacecraft, wagons drawn by animals, boats, strange machines I couldn't figure out, beings on bicycles, and thousands of people on skateboards.

I had seen a few strange aliens, mostly at Alfred's time-space root beer stand, but the sheer number and variety of weird-looking creatures along Good Intentions Boulevard was mind-blowing. There were seemingly intelligent life-forms ranging from the size of a chipmunk to one we saw as big as a blue whale. And species resembling humanoids, reptiles, birds, hunks of rock, and animated pizzas—scaly, slimy, hairy, smooth, lighter than air, glow-in-the-dark, little green men—they were all there, every kind of freak in any number of universes.

"It looks just like places in New Jersey," Freddie said.

"Only more so," Borgel said. "Hell is the most popular place there is."

A really enormous sign came into view. It was incredible. There were lights of every color. Little red animated devils ran all around the edges of it, and real fireworks exploded in the air above it. It was the greatest sign I ever saw. Letters twenty feet high flashed one message after another:

THIS IS IT!

HELL!

THE ORIGINAL—THE ONLY!

HELL!

GET FRIED!

FREE ASBESTOS FOOTWEAR!

HELL!

The Gates of Hell, when we got to them, were even more impressive than the sign. Really fantastic. Made of metal, with all sorts of fancy sculpture on them. Inside, past the gates, there was a fireworks display going on, even better than the one above the sign. There was quite a smell of gunpowder.

Outside the Gates of Hell was a guy with horns! He was capering around and waving the cars in.

"Is that the actual devil?" I asked Borgel.

"Probably just a minor one," Borgel said. "I hear they have quite a few."

"What happens inside?" I asked.

"I'm not exactly sure," Borgel said. "But I know one thing about it."

"What's that?"

"If you didn't like it, you'd have a lot of trouble getting your money back."

We were hung up for quite a while, in front of the Gates of Hell, while traffic from the other direction made left turns in front of us. Most of the cars on Good Intentions Boulevard seemed to be going to Hell.

"Let's just go in for a while," Fafner said. "I want to see what goes on."

"Nah," Borgel said. "I always avoid cheap tourist attractions."

"Besides," Freddie said, "we have someplace important to go."

"It looks great!" Fafner said. "I wish I were going to Hell."

"May your wish be granted," I said.

Once we got past the Gates of Hell, traffic in our direction was much lighter, and we drove along at a reasonable speed. The roadside establishments were much the same, plenty of malls and drive-ins, and places that sold little cement statues—mostly of devils—the kind people put on their lawns.

After a while, we appeared to be getting into the outskirts of Hell. The junk architecture thinned out quite a bit, and we could barely smell the brimstone.

"Maybe we missed the Blue Moon Rest," Freddie said.

"Nah, I was looking carefully," Borgel said. "It ought to be coming up fairly soon now."

(23)

The Blue Moon Rest was a circular building, painted blue. It looked sort of old and beaten-up and friendly. There were a few assorted vehicles parked outside. We went in, and sat down at a table.

There wasn't a humanoid in the place. Various creatures of various shapes and sizes were munching, gnawing, sucking, gobbling, and absorbing plates of great-looking food. I realized that I hadn't been getting many balanced meals lately.

"We are going to eat something, aren't we?" I asked Borgel.

"Of course, Melvin," Borgel said. "After nothing but onions for the last day or so, I think we're all ready for something tasty."

In addition to the tables there was a counter. Behind the counter was an amorphoid fleshopod, flipping hamburgers. He was disgusting, but he didn't approach Alfred in that respect. He didn't affect my appetite one bit. There was a sign hanging above the counter:

OUR SPECIALITY: NO-CAL—NO-NUTE.

FOOD FOR ALL SPECIES.

The waitress came over. She was a fur-bearing Anthropoid from the Nofkis galaxy, Freddie told us. She looked as though she weighed about 450 pounds. Her fur was a light green color—except for which detail, she looked pretty much like any ape at home. She was wearing a button on her uniform that read, *I am the Gorilla of Your Dreams.* She smiled at us. I liked her. She seemed friendly.

"Know what you want, honeys?" the ape waitress asked.

"What's 'no-cal–no-nute,' miss?" Borgel asked.

"No calories, no nutritional content," the waitress said. "We can feed beings from anywhere. All the dishes we prepare are one hundred-percent cellulose. Fiber. Good for man and beast, and whatever. If you desire, we can give you nutrients on the side."

"So what is everything made with, wood chips?" Borgel said.

"I guess," the waitress said. "The maple pancakes are really good, and the okra is real oak."

"I guess I'll have that," Borgel said. "And give me a side of B-complex, some C, E, and trace minerals."

"One humanoid special," the waitress said. "How about you, sweetie?" she said to me.

"I'll have the same, I guess," I said.

"Nothing for me," Fafner said. "I'll have some kibble in the car," he whispered to Borgel.

"And a complimentary synthetic cookie-bone for Rover," the waitress said. "It's on the house, poochie. Enjoy."

"Just a pineburger for me," Freddie said. "And some

iron filings on the side, with maybe some copper sulphate and a slice of lead."

The waitress raised one eyebrow as she wrote down Freddie's order on her pad. "The lead is extra, okay?" she asked.

"Fine," Freddie said.

"Turpentine shakes all around?"

"Just water," Borgel said.

"I'll try the shake," Freddie said.

"Sure you can digest all that?" Borgel asked Freddie. "You and I aren't so young anymore. You might have trouble sleeping."

"I crave minerals," Freddie said. To the waitress, he said, "Your name wouldn't happen to be Milly, would it?"

"That's me, shorty," the ape waitress said.

"I wanted to ask you a question," Freddie said.

"The answer is no, grandpa," Milly said. "I do not date customers. I'm a married gorilla."

"That wasn't it," Freddie said, blushing.

"Oh no?" Milly said. "I saw the way you were giving me the eye. There's no need to be embarrassed. I know I'm irresistably adorable."

"You certainly are," Borgel broke in. "But my companion just wanted to know if your husband, Glugo, has a boat available."

"Could be," Milly said. "Why don't you ask him yourself? Here's the number. The phone's over there." She scribbled a number on a page of her order pad and handed it to Freddie.

"I'll call him right now," Freddie said. "Excuse me."
He went to use the telephone.

When Freddie was gone, Milly said to Borgel, "It's none of my business, but how long have you known that little guy?"

"Not very long," Borgel said.

"Were you aware that he's a Grivnizoid?"

"A Grivnizoid?" Borgel asked.

"A native of the planet Grivnis," Milly said. "Now, I like to think I am not a prejudiced person, but those Grivnizoids can be very dangerous."

"How so?" Borgel asked.

"Well, let's just say they tend to be evil, power mad, untrustworthy, and abominably clever and sneaky. Of course, I could be wrong."

"But you think he's one?"

"How many little bald-headed men you know eat side orders of iron filings and lead?"

"Not many."

"I'd be careful if I were you," Milly said.

"Thanks," Borgel said.

Milly went to give our orders to the fleshopod.

"Do you think she's right?" I asked Borgel.

"She may just be a talkative waitress," Borgel said, "but I have had my doubts about Freddie Nfbnm*. We'll just keep this to ourselves, and Fafner—keep a sharp eye on him, understand?"

"Right, boss," Fafner said.

Freddie came back. "Glugo is going to meet us here," he said.

(24)

The no-cal–no-nute food was actually not bad. It tasted like regular fast-food such as you'd get at any roadside restaurant. Watching Freddie eat the iron filings and lead was a little strange, of course.

"My compliments to the chef!" he called to the Amorphoid Fleshopod behind the counter.

"Merci, monsieur," the fleshopod responded.

Milly came back. "Everything all right here?"

"First rate," Freddie said. "What's for dessert?"

"The maple-walnut ice cream is one hundred percent," Milly said.

"Let's have it," Freddie said.

"Four maple-walnuts," Milly said. "No, five—here comes my sweetie." An ape on a big motorcycle had just pulled up outside the Blue Moon Rest. "Hi, honey!" Milly said to the ape as he came in. He was a big upland gorilla, wearing a blue feed-cap with DON'T MONKEY WITH ME printed on the front.

"Hiya, toots," Glugo said. "Where's the bozo who wants the boat?"

"It's the little goon with the whiskers," Milly said. She

gave Glugo a hug, and I could see her whisper something in his ear. "Sit down. I'll bring you all ice cream and coffeelike substance."

"So?" Glugo said, drumming his fingers on the table. "What can I do for you?"

"We were told you can supply us with a boat," Freddie said.

"For what purpose?" Glugo said.

"Well, we were told about a certain popsicle," Freddie said. "I'm very interested in popsicles."

"Who isn't?" Glugo said. "But you don't need a boat to find one. You can get popsicles everywhere."

"This is a certain particular rather unusual popsicle," Freddie said.

Milly brought the ice cream, which had a strange woody taste. The coffeelike substance was horrible, but I don't like coffee much anyway.

Glugo spooned in ice cream for a while, and drank coffeelike substance with a whistling slurp. "Hmm," he said. "I'm not sure I can help you. Who told you you'd need a boat to find this special popsicle?"

"We were talking to a computer built by a deceased genius named Evil Toad."

"Evil Toad?"

"That's right."

"And the computer he built said you should find me?"

"Yes."

"Mentioned me specifically by name?"

"It said we should ask Milly if you had a boat available.

Also that we'd need a wilderness guide. The computer said maybe you'd take us yourself," Freddie said.

"That's different," Glugo said. "That Popsicle replica knows everything Evil Toad knew and thinks everything he thought."

"So you know about the Great Popsicle replica and computer?" Freddie asked.

"Listen," Glugo said, "I helped build it—the statue part, not the computer. Evil Toad was my best friend. He saved my life once. Nursed me through brain fever. Sat with me day and night while I raved deliriously and plucked at the covers. It's not an easy job taking care of a gorilla with brain fever. I don't forget a thing like that, even if Evil Toad is now just a statue of an ice-pop with an electronic brain. I didn't understand everything Evil thought and did, but if the computer sent you to me, I'll help you, no matter if . . ."

"No matter if what?" Borgel asked.

"Just no matter," Glugo said. "The Popsicle you're looking for lives in the big wilderness on the other side of the river. I'll take you there."

"Lives?" Borgel asked.

"Yes," Glugo said. "But it's shy and elusive. Not more than three beings alive have the skill to track it."

"Are you one of those three?" Freddie asked.

"I've seen it a few times," Glugo said.

"When can we go?" Freddie asked.

"How about right now?" Glugo said. "We can cross the river tonight, sleep on the far shore, and then go looking for the Popsicle. That all right with you geeks?"

"Fine with me," Borgel said. "By the way, what time is it anyway? Seems to me it's been night ever since we arrived."

"It's always night in the region of Hell," Glugo said. "But you'll see daylight across the river. Milly!" he called to his wife. "Pack a bunch of lunches. I'm taking these slobs across the river tonight!"

"You'd better be careful," Milly said.

"I know what I'm doing," Glugo said.

A few minutes later, we were in the Dorbzeldge, following Glugo on his big motorcycle. He turned off Good Intentions Boulevard onto a winding road. We drove after him through the darkness until we came to a low building at the side of a wide dark river.

Glugo switched off his motor and we piled out of the Dorbzeldge.

"Boobs, this is the Styx, a famous river. Maybe you've heard of it," Glugo said.

"Where's the boat?" Freddie asked.

"Right over here," Glugo said. "You fellows don't mind doing some rowing, do you?"

Glugo pulled a flashlight out of his pocket, and showed us a very large boat tied up to a little dock.

"That's a Roman trireme!" Borgel said.

"Sort of huge, isn't it?" I asked.

"It's the only boat I've got," Glugo said. "The three of you will have your work cut out rowing. I assume the dog can't work an oar."

"Sorry," Fafner said. "That's a trick I never learned."

"The three of us have to row that big thing?" I asked. "What will you do."

"I steer," Glugo said. "And crack the whip."

(25)

Rowing Glugo's Roman trireme across the Styx was
no fun at all. Firstly, the thing was enormous and heavy.
Pulling at my oar felt like the other end of the thing was
stuck in semisolid glue. Also with three rowers—Freddie
and I on one side and Borgel on the other—the boat
tended to slew to one side.

It would have been a lot easier if Glugo had rowed, too,
but he seemed to think it was important to stand at the
bow and crack a big whip and holler, "Pull! Pull!" He
said it was important to observe traditions.

By the time we bumped into the opposite shore, I was
exhausted. Apparently, so were Freddie and Borgel,
because we wrapped ourselves in the ratty blankets
Glugo gave us and fell asleep immediately on the grassy
riverbank.

When we woke up, it was dawn—on our side of the
river. The other side, the Hell side, was shrouded by
clouds as black as night. Our side was beautiful—a soft,
misty morning. There were green hills and forest, and
dewy meadows. I would have felt wonderful, waking up
to such a morning, except for one thing—Glugo and the
boat were gone!

The bags of no-cal–no-nute lunches Milly had packed were piled on top of a flat rock. On one of the bags, Glugo had written a note: Dear Goops, Remembered something I had to do. Look around and have fun. Maybe you'll even find what you're looking for. I'll come back in a day or two. Maybe three. Certainly no more than a week.

"How did he get the boat back across by himself?" I wondered out loud.

"My guess is he used the engine," Borgel said.

"The thing has an engine?" I asked.

"Well, something on board smelled of gasoline," Borgel said. "Didn't you notice?"

"I was so tired after a while, I didn't notice anything," I said. "Fafner! You didn't do any rowing! You weren't exhausted! Why didn't you keep watch?"

"Nobody told me to," Fafner said. "You guys all went to sleep, so I did, too."

"Some dog," I said.

"I didn't know," Fafner said. "What was I supposed to do, read that gorilla's mind?"

"Never mind," Freddie said. "The main thing is, we're here. I'm sure the gorilla will come back for us."

"What if he doesn't?" I asked.

"Maybe we won't need him," Freddie said. "Let's look for the Great Popsicle."

"I suggest we have some breakfast first," Borgel said. "Let's see what Milly packed for us."

Cold no-cal–no-nute hamburgers taste a little like pencils. The added nutrients taste like the graphite part. We didn't spend a long time eating breakfast.

"Now, about looking for the Popsicle," Borgel said. "I suggest we spread out. If anyone sees anything like a popsicle, whistle."

"I can't whistle," Fafner said.

"You go with Freddie," Borgel said. "See that nothing happens to him."

"I'll keep an eye on him," Fafner said.

"That's not necessary," Freddie said.

"Take the dog with you," Borgel said. "He needs the exercise. Besides, he might be useful if you run into danger. Melvin and I will go up that hill. You two can take a look in the forest."

"Fine with me," Freddie said. "We'll meet back here about noon to eat some lunch, and see if Glugo has returned."

Borgel and I started up the hill.

"Now that we're alone, there are a lot of questions I want to ask you," I said.

"Not yet," Borgel whispered. "Wait until we're farther away. Grivnizoids have excellent hearing."

"Then he *is* a Grivnizoid?"

"Shh!"

When Borgel thought we had gotten far enough away from Freddie and Fafner, he stopped and sat down on the grassy slope of the hill. "Now, I think we can speak freely," he said. "You wanted to ask questions?"

"I hardly know where to begin," I said. "Who or what is Freddie? What is this popsicle thing we're looking for? Is it real? Is it here? Why does Freddie want to find it so much? Why did Glugo leave us here, and is he coming back?"

"Ha! Good questions! I will answer them all at once, in no particular order. Get comfortable."

I got comfortable.

"First, the Popsicle. It is probably a real thing, but its form is provisional, okay?"

"Nope. Don't understand."

"It's complicated. Certain objects—we'll call them objects, but they're really complex phenomena involving energy, consciousness, time, matter, and other stuff we don't understand—these certain objects appear from time to time."

"What do they do? I mean what are they for?"

"They energize. You know the way our sun energizes our solar system? Everything depends on it. These objects—let's call them energy bundles—energize all sorts of things, maybe a galaxy, or many galaxies, or the known universe."

"Are there a lot of them?"

"There are twenty-six of them."

"How do you know that?"

"I know. Anyway, I think this Popsicle is one of them."

"But why is it a popsicle? I mean, when you think about it, that's sort of a stupid thing to be, isn't it?"

"No more stupid than anything else," Borgel said. "Why is the Sun a flaming gas-ball? Why not an enormous bowl of spaghetti? Why not a grizzly bear or a soft-drink machine? If all your life, the source of life and energy had been a huge blazing soft-drink machine, you'd be used to it. You wouldn't give it a second thought."

"I think it's better for it to be a star," I said.

"I do, too—but really, couldn't that just be because we're used to it? Anyway, I doubt the energy cluster is a popsicle all the time. It's probably one just for now, just for us."

"Why?"

"Maybe Evil Toad knew the answer to that. It's funny how interconnected things are. Someone's vision of something can affect the reality for others. I'll give a concrete example: You know who was it, Napoleon?"

"Yes, he was that French guy."

"Right. Here's a dime." Borgel handed me a dime. "Now, you may also remember that Napoleon was a little shrimp type, a shorty. You read that somewhere?"

"Yes."

"Now. Suppose someone was a time traveler and had the power to change Napoleon to an eight-foot giant."

"Is that possible?"

"Theoretically, sure. If someone did that, and Napoleon was an eight-foot giant, what do you suppose would happen?"

"He'd have to have all his suits lengthened?"

"Not only that. Also, nature would adjust to the change by giving him giant ancestors. That's a temporal adjustment. It's the way things work. Time is elliptical, you remember."

"The bagel?"

"Yes."

"I thought that was space."

"Space, time, it's all the same thing. If you change something here, it connects with things there—in time, in space, in the present, in the future, in the past."

"So why is it a popsicle?"

"I have no idea, but there's a reason, you can be sure of that—just we'll probably never know it. Next, Freddie. You wanted to know about Freddie."

"Yes. Is he a Grivnizoid?"

"I think it's likely. That ape waitress sees a lot of different life-forms, and she thought so. So, assuming he is one, what would he want with the Popsicle, you want to know. If the Popsicle really is one of the twenty-six immensely powerful energy bundles that maintain the shape and quality of reality, he'd want to get it so he could steal its power."

"Why would he do that?"

"So he can be the absolute ruler of everything."

"Freddie?"

"Don't let appearances fool you. If Freddie is a Grivnizoid, he's in disguise. Grivnizoids are big scary fellows. They're just the sort who would want power over the whole universe, and more if possible."

"If he got it, that would be bad," I said.

"Bad for some. Good for Grivnizoids."

"Shouldn't we stop him? What if he finds it?" I asked Borgel.

"Well, I think it may not be so easy to get. Those powerful energy bundles must be very smart. Besides, I doubt that it's here."

"You do?"

"When we get to the top of this hill, I bet you my lunch, we'll find we're on an island. Can't get off. And Glugo . . ."

"Yes, what about Glugo?"

"He's probably gone for help. He certainly knows that Freddie is likely to try something dangerous. Glugo seemed to be a good ape—what do you think?"

It was just a few yards to the top of the hill. I ran ahead, and when I got there, I could see river on all sides.

"It *is* an island," I said.

Borgel arrived at the top of the hill. "See? What did I tell you? Glugo stranded us here, and he's probably getting in touch with someone with the authority to call Freddie off."

"Who can do that?"

"Oh, a number of people. Probably he'll get in touch with somebody like Rolzup, the Martian High Commissioner."

"I've heard of him," I said.

"I'm not surprised. He's a very important person."

"So why didn't you do something to stop Freddie yourself?" I asked Borgel.

"It's not my style," Borgel said. "Remember, Freddie is just doing what's normal—if you happen to be a Grivnizoid. I try not to judge people or interfere. Besides, I find that things usually work out pretty well if I leave them alone. I don't think there's any real danger."

"No danger? From what you've told me, not that I understand most of it, if Freddie could somehow steal the power of the Great Popsicle, he'd be the most powerful being in the universe!"

"At least."

"So why not dangerous?"

"Well, for one thing, Freddie isn't all that bad—oh, maybe ruthless and power mad and possibly a little cruel, but in a cute sort of way. What's more, who's to say he's going to find the Popsicle? We're on this island, and the Popsicle is probably all the way over on the far shore."

"What's that?" I asked.

"What?" Borgel asked.

"That thing down there," I said.

"You mean that thing romping in the grass?"

"Yes."

"That thing that is glowing with an amazing light?"

"Yes, that thing."

"Very pretty, isn't it?"

"What is it?"

"Looks a little like a popsicle."

"Are you sure?" I asked Borgel.

"It's hard to tell at this distance," Borgel said. "What we need is a pair of binoculars."

"But we don't have any," I said.

"I have a good pair, made by Carl Flutz," Borgel said. "Maybe I should just nip back and get them."

"Nip back where?" I asked. "Remember the Dorbzeldge is on the other side of the river."

"They're not in the Dorbzeldge. They're in my room. I think I'll get them. Wait here and watch that thing while I'm gone."

"Oh no! You've gone mushy in the head! You can't get your binoculars from your room! We're away off in time-space-and-the-other, remember?"

"Ah-ha! There are plenty of tricks you don't know," Borgel said. "Just watch this."

Borgel put one finger up his nose, another finger in his ear, and whistled shrilly. Then he vanished—just ceased to be—was gone—turned into thin air. I felt a sinking feeling. I thought maybe he'd been bilboked again. I didn't have time to get upset, because in a few seconds, there was another whistle, and he was back, with a pair of old field glasses.

"Just where I thought they were," Borgel said.

"Wait a second!" I shouted. "Where did you get those?"

"Where I said," Borgel said. "They were in my room."

"You just went back to your room, in our apartment, and came back here in, what, ten seconds?"

"Sure. I told you, there are tricks."

"Can I do that, too?"

"Why not?"

I was astonished. "So we could have gotten anywhere without driving in the Dorbzeldge?"

"Yes," Borgel said. "But what fun would that be? Here, I brought you some fig bars."

He handed me a cellophane bag of fig bars.

"Where is that thing?" Borgel asked, peering through the binoculars.

"I don't know. I forgot all about it," I said.

"Hmm. Seems to have gone out of sight," Borgel said.

"Hand me a couple of fig bars, will you?"

Freddie and Fafner came puffing up the hill. "We heard a whistle," Freddie said.

"Where did you get the fig bars?" Fafner asked.

"Borgel found them," I said, handing him one.

"Well, did you see something?" Freddie asked.

"I thought I did," Borgel said, "but I don't see it now."

(26)

"What was it like, the thing you saw?" Freddie asked.

"Little," Borgel said.

"Couldn't have been the Great Popsicle," Freddie said. "It has to be huge. Remember the replica?"

"Oh yes," Borgel said. "That replica was pretty big, wasn't it?"

"I wish you'd take this search more seriously," Freddie said. "Look, we can see everything from up here. Nothing like a gigantic popsicle in sight. It must be in the forest. Say! We're on an island!"

"I was wondering when you'd notice," Borgel said.

"That makes it better," Freddie said. "If it's here, it can't get away from us. I'm going back to the forest. Who's coming with me?"

"Fafner, help Freddie," Borgel said.

"I'm tired," Fafner said.

"Go anyway. We'll look around here some more, and catch up with you."

Freddie and Fafner went down the hill toward the forest.

"Don't whistle unless you're sure!" Freddie called back.

"Ha!" Borgel said to me. "I'm not sure Freddie really knows what he's looking for."

"Why do you say that," I asked.

"Well, there's no reason the Great Popsicle has to be huge," he said. "If it's an entity of enormous power, as I suspect, it could be of atomic size, or as big as a world—or anything in between, anytime it likes. Similarly, if it wanted to get off this island, or eat this island, or turn this island into a fig bar, it could do it."

"Wow!" I said.

"That's what I meant when I said it might not be so easy to catch," Borgel said. "I think he's heard something about it, but maybe doesn't really know what he's up against. It's a little like trying to catch an elephant with a butterfly net, which I have seen done once or twice, but it's not the best way."

"Would it do any of those things?" I asked.

"What things?"

"Turn this island into a fig bar, and things like that?"

"It could," Borgel said. "But would it? Here. Look through these. See whether you think it would."

"It's back?" I asked.

"Right over there," Borgel pointed. "Adjust the focus with the little knob in the middle."

We were lying prone, just below the crest of the hill. I steadied myself on my elbows and looked through the binoculars.

I had to scan around a bit, and then I saw it. There wasn't any doubt in my mind. It was something powerful—as powerful as the Sun, or a whole lot of suns—and it was a popsicle. It was sort of prancing around in the grass, as though it were playing. It was an orange popsicle, maybe a little larger than an ordinary one. It seemed to be alive, and—this is the unbelievable part—it was beautiful. I know that seems idiotic, to say a popsicle can be beautiful, but this one was. It was not that it was much different from thousands of popsicles I'd seen—except for the amazing light that seemed to come from it. It was beautiful in a way nothing I had ever seen or thought of was beautiful.

"Unusual, isn't it?" Borgel said.

I wanted to laugh. Or cry. I knew I could never figure out what was causing all these strong feelings in me. I wanted to stay there, looking at the shining Popsicle forever. It gave me shivers and made me feel warm, the way you feel when you're bathed with sunlight.

"Uncle Borgel, what? . . . I mean, why? . . . I mean, it's got some power. I can feel it. It isn't bad. It's good. I don't understand what I'm feeling."

"It's love, sonnyboy," Borgel said. "You're feeling what the Popsicle is putting forth. Energy and love, and a whole lot of it. That's why I never worry. It's impossible to persuade anybody of it until they see it for themselves, but most of the big things in the universe—like that beautiful little Popsicle—are like that."

"Most things in the universe love us?"

"That's what I've observed," Borgel said, thoughtfully nibbling a fig bar.

"Gee."

"Yeh, nice isn't it? Now wait. Pretty soon the Popsicle is going to be sure we don't have any hostile feelings."

"Then what?" I asked.

"Who knows? Wait and see."

We waited. Pretty soon the Popsicle came closer to us. The closer it got, the more I liked it. It was wonderful watching the Popsicle move around in the grass. It was like dancing. When it came closer still, it was like dancing and music. Also like a light show. Also like hearing music. Wonderful music. It was also like riding a ride at an amusement park. The Popsicle was dancing all around us, but it felt as though we were moving, dancing with it.

I also felt that all of a sudden I knew a lot of things I never knew before, strange things that were hard to put into words. I felt that I was part of something larger than I could have even imagined a few minutes before—something that included everything and everyone that existed or had ever existed or ever would exist. I felt that the universe was wise, and as part of the universe, I was wise, too.

"This is the greatest thing that ever happened to me," I said to Borgel.

"You bet, sonnyboy," Borgel said. "What's more, once it starts happening, it never really stops."

"That's a little scary," I said. "About all I can do is sit here with my jaw hanging open. I don't know if I could handle it going on all the time."

"Oh, it doesn't go on all the time like this," Borgel said. "Most of the time, it's just a little vibration you're aware of—but you're always partly aware. Just being this close to something like that Popsicle is a little intense."

"And yet, we're able to carry on this normal conversation while all that power is going on," I said.

"We always do everything while all that power is going on," Borgel said. "Only most people don't notice it."

"How can they not notice it?" I asked. "It's like ten orchestra concerts, six fireworks displays, an earthquake, and a rock concert all at once."

"As I said, it isn't usually this obvious," Borgel said. "But it's pretty obvious. There is no limit to what most people don't notice. Look, it's moving away."

The Popsicle was skipping away into the distance. I really loved that Popsicle. I'd have thought I'd be sorry to see it go, but I wasn't. I somehow knew that it would always be with me in some way or other.

"Boy!" I said. "That's remarkable."

"I'm glad you got to experience it," Borgel said. "You'll be a better person now that you know a little more about how things really are."

"Freddie's mistaken if he thinks he can catch that thing," I said.

"Maybe we're mistaken about Freddie," Borgel said. "Anyway, you see why I'm not worried."

(27)

We sat on the top of the hill, nibbling the last of the fig bars. I was thinking about what I had seen and experienced. It was quiet and the sun was shining.

I was different than I had been before I saw the Popsicle. I wasn't a whole lot different—I still felt like me—but something had changed, I was sure of that. I noticed that things looked different to me. Colors were different. It was as if things had not been in full color before, and now they were. And I felt something inside me that I hadn't been aware of before. It was like a place in the middle of me, quiet and active both at once.

"So?" Borgel said. "Now do you understand everything?"

"I feel like I do," I said.

"Yetz?"

"But I don't."

"Good. Poifect. Maybe you have some questions?"

"Yes."

"What?"

"Is the Popsicle God?"

"Sure."

"It is?"

"Everything is. Everything is God."

"I knew that," I said. But now I knew it better. "So let me get it straight, just to be sure."

"Okay," Borgel said.

"The Popsicle is a . . . a . . ."

"Manifestation."

"Manifestation . . . of some sort of great power."

"Yep," Borgel said, shaking the last fig bar crumbs out of the cellophane bag into his mouth.

"You say there are a number of these."

"Correct. I heard there are twenty-six of them, but it doesn't matter. There could only be one, there could be more."

"It doesn't have to be a popsicle—it could appear as anything. It's just a popsicle sort of by accident."

"And because a popsicle is as good a way for us to see it as anything else."

"And this Popsicle sort of . . . well, watches over everything, and gives everything the power to work and exist and do stuff."

"Yaas," Borgel said, "I guess that's a good enough explanation."

"And it loves us."

"Certainly seems that way."

"Why?"

"Why?"

"Why does it love us?" I asked.

"Why not? I suppose that's just the sort of popsicle it is," Borgel said.

"It sure is neat," I said.

"I think so, too," Borgel said.

Fafner appeared. He seemed excited and out of breath.

"Fafner! Where's Freddie?" Borgel asked.

"He's in the forest," Fafner said.

"Something happened?"

"Hoo boy!" Fafner said.

"So why didn't you whistle? I told you to whistle."

"I told you, I can't whistle!" Fafner said. "I'm a dog, for Pete's sake!"

"You could have barked."

"Oh. Barked." Fafner looked embarrassed.

"Well, what is it?"

"He changed."

"Who changed? Freddie?" Borgel asked.

"Freddie. Changed."

"Changed how?"

"Changed all over," Fafner said. "He changed into a monster! A big one! A scary one!"

"No fooling!" Borgel said. "Did he change into something between an octopus and a gnarled old tree?"

"Yes! With eyestalks and really bad breath," Fafner said. "How did you know?"

"That's a Grivnizoid. That's how they look. They're good at disguising themselves—and you can see why they'd want to."

"Well, he's undisguised himself now," Fafner said.

"That must have surprised you," Borgel said. "I wonder why he did it."

"There's more," Fafner said.

"Tell us the more," Borgel said.

"We saw the Popsicle," Fafner said. "It was amazing! I tell you, it was the nicest little Popsicle! I just loved it."

"We saw it, too," I said.

"Cutest, sweetest little Popsicle," Fafner said.

"Yeh, it's adorable," Borgel said. "How did Freddie like it?"

"Too much," Fafner said. "I think he may have eaten it."

"Whoops!" Borgel said.

(28)

"Oh no!" I shouted. "Then Freddie, a Grivnizoid, is the most powerful thing in the universe!"

"You're sure he ate it?" Borgel asked.

"Not sure," Fafner said. "I didn't want to get too close. In fact, I was busy running away. But it looked like that—and there were some very ugly noises."

"I'll bet there were," Borgel said.

"We're doomed," I said.

"Never say doomed," Borgel said.

"What should I say?" I asked.

"Say 'in terrible trouble,'" Borgel said. "But it remains to be seen whether we are. Let's go see."

"I was going to suggest we try to swim to shore," Fafner said.

"No, I think we'd better find out what's been going on," Borgel said.

We started down the hill. Near the beach we ran into Glugo, with about fifteen other apes.

"Glugo!" I shouted.

"Where's the little guy?" Glugo asked.

"We think he's a Grivnizoid," Borgel said.

"That's what I was afraid of," Glugo said. "That's why I went for help."

"Who are these apes?" Borgel asked.

"These are the members of the Greater Hades Motorcycle Club," Glugo said. "They're tough guys. I'll introduce you later. Now, we'd better find the Grivnizoid before he figures out that the Great Popsicle is on the far side of the river."

"There's a problem about that," Borgel said.

"What?"

"When last seen, the Popsicle was here, on the island."

"Zeus!" Glugo said, slapping his forehead with the palm of his hand. "Now we're in terrible trouble!"

"See?" Borgel said to me. To Glugo he said, "Fafner was the last one to see them. We were just going to have a look."

"Let's go!"

Borgel and Glugo and the members of the ape motorcycle club and I followed Fafner toward the forest. When we got there it was deathly quiet.

We followed Fafner, who was walking on tiptoe. We all walked on tiptoe, too, and whispered.

"This could be bad," Glugo whispered.

"Let's wait and see," Borgel whispered back.

"They were right around here somewhere," Fafner whispered.

There was nothing in sight.

"Spread out," Glugo whispered to the members of the G.H.M.C. "No, stay together—keep a sharp lookout and don't make any noise."

We tiptoed through the forest, keeping a sharp lookout and not making any noise.

Then we saw it! In a clearing, a little distance away, we saw what had to be Freddie. My first Grivnizoid.

Keep in mind that in my travels in space and time, I had already encountered a Bloboform, an Amorphoid Fleshopod, and quite a number of life-forms which would appear to the average person to be scary, dangerous, and nauseating. The Grivnizoid beat them all. By a light year. It was huge. It was powerful-looking. It seemed alert, and it was built for combat.

"I have to tell you," Borgel whispered to Glugo, "Fafner thinks Freddie may have eaten the Popsicle."

"Buddha!" Glugo whispered between his teeth. "I shudder to think what that could mean for intelligent life-forms everywhere."

We were creeping closer to the monstrous thing. I didn't know why we were doing that. What we should have been doing would have been to run the other way as fast as we could. There wasn't any question that the Grivnizoid could eat the sixteen gorillas, Borgel, Fafner, and me for lunch. The only question was, was it powerful enough to have eaten the Popsicle?

"The only question is," Glugo said, "is it powerful enough to have eaten the Popsicle?"

"Let's find out," Borgel said. He stood up straight, walked directly toward the Grivnizoid, stopped just a few yards from it, and shouted, "Hey, Freddie! Did you eat the Popsicle?"

The Grivnizoid turned slowly toward Borgel. Only

then did I see its face. I wished I hadn't. It moved almost like some enormous plant, or as though it were underwater. From deep within the huge body, I heard a faint voice I recognized as Freddie's.

"Yes," it said.

"That was your plan, all along?" Borgel asked.

"Yes."

"Why did you want to do it?" Borgel asked.

"To get . . . power," the Grivnizoid said haltingly.

"So? Now how do you feel?" Borgel asked.

"Funny . . . you . . . should . . . ask," the Grivnizoid said. "Ordinarily . . . I . . . can . . . digest . . . anything."

"And this time?"

"Uurrp," the Grivnizoid belched.

Borgel turned to the rest of us. "Come closer, gentlemen—and apes. I suggest we sit quietly and watch while Freddie digests his snack."

Glugo whispered in Borgel's ear, "It seems weak. Maybe this would be a good time to attack it."

"I strongly advise you to do no such thing," Borgel said. "Just sit down and watch for a while."

The apes, Borgel, Fafner, and I sat in a semicircle on the forest floor while Freddie the Grivnizoid appeared to be struggling with a monumental case of indigestion.

We said nothing. Now and then the Grivnizoid burped.

Time passed.

As we sat, watching, I had plenty of time to study Freddie in his Grivnizoid form. As I said, he was hideous, a complete departure from the form in which I'd known him up to now, which was on the cute side. The fact that as a Grivnizoid he was dealing with profound gastric distress didn't make his appearance any more pleasant.

And yet, I found I was getting used to him. After a time, I even found that I didn't have to avert my eyes occasionally, or concentrate on not being sick. In fact, a little while later, I was amazed to realize that I was beginning to actually like his looks.

The apes seemed to be more comfortable, too. Their expressions had softened, and they were looking at Freddie with something approaching pleasure.

Fafner had gone to sleep, with a peaceful look on his face, and Borgel was quite calm, humming little tunes to himself.

"You know," I said to him, "this is crazy, but I can't help feeling that Freddie isn't such a bad guy."

"No, he really isn't," Borgel said. "Keep sitting a while, and you'll see something good."

Freddie was feeling better, I could tell. I was glad he was finally getting over his upset stomach. This struck me as weird because, after all, I had come to love the little Popsicle so much—but then, I loved Freddie, too. That last thought tripped me up. "Loved Freddie?" How truly bizarre.

But it was so. I realized the others were feeling the same thing.

Freddie was feeling fine now. He was up on his tentacles, sort of hopping around. It was grotesque, but at the same time, a pleasure to watch. He was also looking quite . . . well, pretty. There was a fascinating glow coming from him.

I got it. "Well, I'll be doggoned," I said to Borgel. "Freddie has turned into what the Popsicle was."

"Absotoomlutely," Borgel said. "What, you thought anything else could happen?"

Freddie was up and dancing now. It was the same dance the Popsicle had done. Actually it was a little better, because Freddie, with all those tentacles, could do some moves the Popsicle couldn't. The apes had all caught on, too. It was the whole performance Borgel and I had seen on the hilltop, all over again.

"It's just as good as before!" I said to Borgel.

"Better," Borgel said. "Just think, now the wonderful energy thing is someone who was once a personal friend of ours."

"Hey, Freddie!" I shouted. "What does it feel like?"

But he was too involved in being a supremely powerful energy bundle to be able to answer, and soon after that, he pranced away into the forest.

Glugo and the members of the ape motorcycle club were deliriously happy.

"So," Glugo said. "We didn't need to protect the Popsicle after all."

"Nah," Borgel said. "It's more like the other way around."

"Well, come on back with us to the Blue Moon Rest," Glugo said. "We'll have a party."

The party was still going on when Borgel, Fafner, and

I said good-bye to Milly, Glugo, and the G.H.M.C., and drove off in the Dorbzeldge.

In the Dorbzeldge I asked Borgel, "So Freddie will just go on being a Popsicle—I mean a whatever he is?"

"Probably for a long time," Borgel said. "Until he changes. Everything changes. One thing is sure—not many creatures will try to eat him."

"Was that what he wanted?" I asked. "I mean, when he wanted to get the power of the Popsicle, did he know this would happen to him?"

"Probably not," Borgel said. "I always thought he didn't have a very clear idea of what the Popsicle was, but he does now, hee hee hee."

"I'm going to take a nap," I said.

"Good idea," Borgel said. "I'll drive awhile."

I slept right past the Gates of Hell, and the two-dimensional monochrome state of existence. In fact, I didn't wake up until we were in a place I recognized.

"Hey!" I said, "we're right near Hapless Toad's place."

"So we are," Borgel said. "Let's stop in and see him."

We drove up the long path through the forest until we came to the round building. Everything was the same, including Hapless Toad sleeping in his old car.

"Fifty zlotys to go in, and the dog stays in the car," he said.

"Hapless Toad, don't you remember us?" I asked.

"Sure I remember you," Hapless Toad said. "What do you think, that entitles you to a discount?"

"Why'd you want to see him again?" I asked Borgel.

"Well, I really wanted to see the replica," Borgel said.

We paid Hapless Toad our hundred zlotys and walked up to the building which housed the replica. The sign had been changed. It now read, THE GREAT GRIVNIZOID.

Inside was a life-size replica of Freddie.

"How is this possible?" I asked Borgel.

"Ask the Grivnizoid," Borgel said.

"How long have you been a Grivnizoid?" I asked the replica.

"I have always been a Grivnizoid," the computer replica said.

"But there used to be a statue of a popsicle here," I said.

"Is that a question?"

". . . wasn't there?" I added.

"Yes."

"So how come it's changed?"

"A temporal adjustment," the replica said. "You know that Napoleon was a little shrimpish guy, right? Well imagine that some being went back in time, and changed him to an eight-foot giant. Well, if that happened . . ."

"I get it," I said to Borgel. "Let's go."

Outside I said to Hapless Toad, "How do you like the replica now that it's a Grivnizoid?"

"It's always been a Grivnizoid," Hapless Toad said.

We got back into the Dorbzeldge.

"Well, where to next?" Borgel asked.

"Home!" Fafner said. "I've been missing all my favorite TV shows."

Borgel turned to me. "What do you say, Mr. Experienced Time Tourist; you ready to go home for a while?"

"For a while," I said.